DARKEST
W(the)OLVES

The Secrets of Shifters Series

A.K. Koonce

The Darkest Wolves

Copyright 2020 A.K. Koonce

All Rights Reserved

Editing by Polished Perfection

Cover design by Sanja's Covers

No portion of this book may be reproduced in any form without express written permission from the author. Any unauthorized use of this material is prohibited.

This is a work of fiction. Names, characters, places, and incidents either are the products of the author's imagination or are used fictitiously. Any resemblance to actual persons, living or dead, businesses, companies, events, or locales is entirely coincidental.

 Created with Vellum

CONTENTS

1. That Crazy Bitch	1
2. A Simple Choice	8
3. The Plot	17
4. The Kingdom of Hell	28
5. Puppy Training	53
6. Touch Me	64
7. Brothers	70
8. It's Getting Hard	79
9. Wake-Up Call	87
10. That Panty Intuition	92
11. Dueling Seduction	97
12. The Plot Thickens	105
13. Then There Were Three	113
14. Shit	133
15. A Losing Winner	138
16. The Time Has Come	146
A Note From the Author	161
Taming	163
Also by A.K. Koonce	173
About A.K. Koonce	177

ONE

THAT CRAZY BITCH

"The crazy wild bitch is finally becoming a crazy married bitch," my cousin Lisah murmurs to her mother, as if I can't hear her sneers from behind me.

I broke her nose when we were seven. It still leans on her pudgy face just a fraction of an inch to the left. The kids used to call her Lazy-Nosed Lisah because of it. To be honest, I still do when I need cheering up from time to time.

When I glare at her in the full-length mirror, I know she and I are both sharing that fond memory.

"I wish I was as beautiful as you on my mating day," Nyra whispers with a soft smile on her plump lips. She's good at ignoring Lisah. At ignoring any nasty words really. So damn good it makes me wonder if all of my anger is to make up for her abundance of disgustingly pure happy thoughts.

She's pretty. Wholesome. Soft hair like the sun, and

eyes as dark as the night. She's a muted appearance of myself really. Our lips, they're the same though. I see myself in her when she smiles, even if I'm not naïve enough to feel the happiness she feels every single day of her sweet life.

Because the Goddess Moon blessed Nyra with kindness.

A woman's life as a wolf shifter has many rites of passage. At thirteen, we become a woman, a real member of our pack's society. And during the blessings of that celebration, a mage of nature comes and connects us to our Goddess. One gift is all we're given to guide us in this life.

I remember wishing like hell for the gift of intelligence. Or strength like my mother. Or even some fucking poise to help me with the battle training I once did with my father.

The possibilities are endless. The blessings of our Goddess Moon know no bounds.

And that's why I was blessed with *beauty*.

A fucking face.

That's what the Goddess gave me. A flawless complexion where others got bravery. A nice ass while my neighbors flaunted their wit, innovation, and perseverance.

I mean, sure, my pants fit great, but would it have killed the Goddess to wonder if I might need something more than filling out a good pair of trousers?

The sigh that blows from my lungs fans the pale locks

hanging in perfect curls around my features. The hair my mother is braiding here and there hangs down to the waist of my sheer mating gown.

Today's the day...

Cue the fireworks.

And depression.

The females around me idly gossip. The chatter is endless and grates against my mind. Of course, they talk about Mika. He'll be a good mate. A strong man who should fulfill his duty to me and load my uterus up with litters and litters of pups to make our pack proud.

Yes, my uterus is one lucky bitch indeed. Listen to her rave about the thought of waddling around and crying constantly about the way her left hip hurts when it waddles a bit too fast:

Silence. My uterus is fucking silent.

Because it's in mourning, let's face it.

"Cersia, you're going to be glowing once you're pregnant. You'll finally experience true happiness," my cousin, Lisah, says to smooth things over.

"You'll do our pack proud," my mother agrees.

"Indeed, I will truly spread my legs with honor," I say before I can stop myself.

I feel my lips tense up in that way they always do when I try to force a smile. The women look at my blank look of lunacy with the flat tilt at the corner of my plump red lips.

"Oh," Aunt Helana whispers slowly like realization

just bitch-slapped every one of them at the same damn time.

Shit. I didn't smile right... Why does my face do that? Why?

"Glowing. Definitely." I nod to try to ease the tragic look of worry every single one of them is tossing my way. "I will glow so fucking hard," I add before trailing that thought off into tense silence. "I'm going to lie down." I finally let it go while staring at them in the mirror, but I can see the damage is done.

I say nothing for a beat longer, and during that time, Lisah whispers something about *crazy* once more to Aunt Helana. She always has to drop the C word around me.

The cunt.

My eyes narrow on the round woman, and her mouth snaps shut in an instant, because my mother will never tell them my one hidden secret. Instead, she'll warn them every day of their lives about my *temper*.

It's a fiery thing, she tells them.

And she's not wrong.

There are no more words to say. Nothing I can say could explain why I'm not overjoyed Mika picked me. Even when I'm not speaking, I'm still screwing life up.

It's not my fault.

I told father I wanted to join our leaders. Or at the very least, I wanted to become a Fighter Wolf and keep our pack safe. I told them all what I'd hoped for in life.

But father died.

And I'm too pretty to waste the Goddess's gifts.

A beautiful face isn't meant for politics or war.

Sometimes I wonder if it would hurt less to hear that praise of my features if I'd known beauty as a friend my entire life.

But I didn't. I didn't grow up pretty. I grew up sturdy and brutish like my father. I was always his little shadow trying to be just like papa.

Then one day, I was beautiful. My mother emphasized it and told everyone daily. And I'd never realized how much it hurt to know I wasn't before.

I was oblivious to my chubby cheeks and soft adolescent belly. I was blind to that unwanted appearance. Until everyone reminded me day in and day out: *Ceria, you're so beautiful. Your mother must be so proud. You're going to make a man very lucky one day.*

Yes, yes. But imagine if I could keep my mother safe. Or if I could outwit any man. Oh, the things I'd give to outwit Mika to his stupid, brick-like face.

Not that I can't. I certainly can. But damn, Goddess Moon, back me up sometimes.

None of the quiet women stop me as I wander back to my sister's bedroom and shut the door. I sit at the edge of the quilted mattress for a long time and consider my options.

The thing is, I don't have any. I can only do my duty as a woman and mate with Mika to keep a family secret kept very far in the dark.

It was my father's burden, and now it is my own.

And I'll carry it just as he did: crying and bitching every step of the way.

So I stare out the little square window on the far wall of the cottage and wait for the dread to ease into acceptance. I wait. And I wait. And I wait.

An hour passes as the sun settles low in the pale blue sky, and my stomach still turns sickly. My teeth are still clenched tightly.

And the inky black shadow pacing at the tree line is still watching me.

He's my one distraction from all of this.

He's a stranger. The black-haired wolf hidden in the brush isn't one of ours. Darker wolves are an ominous sighting in our pack. They're as rare as dragons nowadays. Wolves like this don't come here. They're not our kind.

The darkness of the creature alone feels like an omen.

How very ironic that I'd see the hellish creature on my perfect little mating day. The Goddess hates me indeed.

The brutish beast has held eyes with me for several minutes now. The mass of him alone is frightening. I should be scared. He looks like a pet of the devil himself. And yet, all I do is hold his glaring gaze.

Neither of us move.

Then, as if tiring of our game, his front paw motions forward, and a puff of dirt billows around his fur where he dares take a step into the line of fading sunlight.

The fucking audacity of this bitch.

I storm across the room, and I'm flinging open the window at once.

"Are you challenging me, Hell Cunt?" I scream into the wind.

Barrley, the old neighbor lady, stops dead in her tracks. A wicker basket of daisies hangs limply in her hand. Her big brown eyes widen while her jaw rears back so far she gives herself several chins, and none of them are pretty.

The young girl at her side whispers beneath her breath, but I hear her quietness.

Crazy, she tells her mother.

"Are you...alright, Cersia?" Barrley asks with a voice that sounds like it's walking on eggshells to even address the crazy woman barking out the window like a feral dog giving a taunting squirrel a good ass-chewing.

My attention shifts from the hesitant woman to the tree line.

But the wolf is gone. Nothing but swaying tree limbs and rustling leaves peer back at me.

And maybe...just maybe I really am the village crazy bitch.

TWO

A SIMPLE CHOICE

The heaviness of the moon presses down on me when my eyes open to the shadowy room. I can't say when I finally gave up the constant dread and let my mind rest, but it seems to have happened. Sleep and a bit of calm found me.

It just didn't last long enough.

Dim lighting dances across the smooth white walls, and the sound of the mating chanting sways in rhythm with the flickering light of the flames that are awaiting me outside.

It's almost time.

In just under an hour, I'll walk out to the highest ground beneath our Goddess Moon, and mate with the one man I'll look to for guidance for the rest of my miserable fucking life.

Sounds real fucking romantic, doesn't it?

At the simple thought of living a long empty life of

lies, my heart pounds harder against my chest. The air caught in my throat fights to fill my lungs.

You'll be safe though... He'll keep you safe...

I should leave.

I should...

I—

A slamming of rattling glass shakes through my anxiety.

I'm on my feet, and the beast inside me is baring its teeth against my lips before I can bite back its snarl. My canines are on full display when I lock gazes with the palest green eyes.

They're like sea glass shimmering in the sunlight. Electric and calming all at the same time.

And yet, the dark wolf peering through the bedroom window is a threat to me.

Stranger, my beast hisses.

A beautiful, beautiful stranger, my mind argues.

The way my molars grind at the sight of the threat sends a painful stabbing straight through my jaw. Every muscle in my body tenses tightly, and as fight or flight soars through my body, my feet are storming toward the asshole before the adrenaline can fully settle in.

The window flings up with the force of my palms, and I'm face-to-face with the smoky wolf, who simply stares me down. I'm less than an inch away from his smooth snout. The heat of his even breath fans against my cheek, and I wait for his move.

Until I'm tired of waiting.

I'm so damn tired of waiting for things to happen in my life.

And this fucker is no different.

"What do you want, Hell Cunt?"

Those pretty shining eyes appraise me in a mocking way that makes my blood boil despite the cool breeze that wafts through my sheer gown.

Two big paws press into the white window frame Boards creak beneath his massive weight.

And then charred black smoke bursts around the creature. His image shatters with explosive sparking magic. It happens so fast I barely catch the scent of ash against his fur.

Then a stunning green-eyed man is sitting lazily in the window frame where a once terrifying beast loomed. The bend of his knee is where he languidly rests one of his arms while he judges me with a sharp gaze. His attention never does dip down to the curves of my body that the moon highlights for anyone who might look my way.

The tight dress is to emphasize the Mating Moon. Tonight, Mika and I are to join as one beneath the light of our Goddess. And by morning, my sheer gown will be tight against a blooming belly. By dawn, I'll be an expecting mother of beautiful pups.

There's absolutely nothing wrong with that.

But it's wrong for me.

It isn't my path, and I know it.

It's so damn distracting that anxious thoughts of marriage are clawing at the back of my mind. Even now in this bizarre moment with this naked man suddenly taking an inventory of my appearance.

And seemingly finding me lacking. Which is just... It's fucking insulting is what it is.

"You're her, huh?" he asks with as much enthusiasm as a dog being offered a plate of lettuce.

I don't like him. I don't like his *fuck you* demeanor. That's my demeanor, and there's only enough room for one bitch in this conversation.

And that's going to have to be me. I've earned it. Just ask Lazy-Nosed Lisah.

My lips part to tell him off, but apparently my hands are quicker.

With one swift shove, my palms collide with smooth rigid shoulders, and the cockiness is pushed right out of him as he goes tumbling down from his high pedestal.

He lands with a thud and a stream of curses that make a real smile almost touch my lips.

Almost.

"What the fuck!?" He's back up in no time with a bit of leaf stuck in his short black hair. Dude might be a total fuck face, but his recovery time is impressive. "The Night Witch said there exists a woman more beautiful than heaven and more pained than hell."

Oh.

That...that does sound like me, doesn't it?

I hide my surprise a bit too late when I close my gaping mouth and cross my arms.

Only then does his attention slip to the outline of my perfection.

My features steel, and I try to get to the point of his conversation before Nyra comes to get me for the Mating Moon.

"And?" I ask harshly.

What does he want? Is he here to see the Goddess's work firsthand? The laziest gift that any shifter has ever been given?

What?

"I just..." He shrugs just lightly then before meeting my eyes with that same look of cold carelessness. "I guess I just expected a more impressive woman. I don't know."

My jaw drops so fast it high fives the floor, and they both celebrate the first real shock I think I've ever experienced in my entire life.

"Excuse the fuck out of me?" My hands hit my hips so hard it hurts, but the outraged sting to my ego hurts more.

Expected a more impressive woman?

Of all the times people sweetly called me pretty, I never thought I'd be demanding it from someone.

And yet, I almost am.

I almost want him to acknowledge all the ways I know I'm beautiful.

Just tell me I'm fucking pretty!

"You *don't* think I'm attractive?" I hold back my irrational anger by barely a thread of dwindling politeness.

He takes a good minute to reassess me with a slow rake of his infuriatingly dead eyes.

I cannot believe I thought his piss green gaze was beautiful.

"I've seen better," he finally spits.

My palm snaps across his mouth like he just threatened me.

He basically did!

He threatened my humbleness.

I'm humble, Goddess dammit!

A sharp smile twists his lips, and his thumb drags across his mouth to wipe away the pain I know I just left him with. Still he sneers at me as if I just complimented him rather than attacked him.

"I have an offer to make you, beautiful," he whispers with a dragging drawl of his low tone.

It's mocking now. That pet name is a mocking insult, and I want to clock my fist against perfect teeth for ever saying a word to me.

He's the rudest fur fucker I've ever had to meet.

My teeth are clenched shut so tightly that I can't even respond to him. A high arch of my eyebrow is as much as I can do.

"You're interested," he says casually, and as he leans in, placing his big hand against the window sill between us, my attention slips down the hard lines of his chest. Lean narrow muscle tone gives him a lithe appearance that says he's quick.

But something in the back of my mind tells me I

could take him if I had to. The skills I've learned from my father have never been wasted.

I'll never waste his legacy.

And I know if I keep talking to this asshole shifter, we'll end up putting those skills to use.

"Come take a walk with me." There's a flawless charisma to his words.

It's like he doesn't recall being a total dick just three minutes ago. He's completely forgotten it. Dicknesia has taken over his mind. It thrusted right in, and now he's just a sweet-talking pussy charmer.

As if my pussy could be so naïve.

A heartbeat pulses between my thighs like a reply, and I hate her betrayal in this moment.

I've never despised a man so fast.

A smile pulls at my lips as I adjust my arms firmer over my chest. When I tilt in close, he leans in too. There's a new glint in his eyes. A sexy, knowing look.

Fuck that look too. As a matter of fact, fuck all of his personalities. None of them are worth a second of my time.

Yet, still he's shifting close to me at the simple thought of me possibly giving in to him. My lips graze his ear. My exhale fans out along his neck just as I finally reply.

"No," I whisper seductively.

My fingers grip the window, and without warning, I slam it down firmly in place between us. Unfortunately, he's quick enough to jerk his fingers away before any damage can be done.

Dammit.

His pretty eyes twitch villainously.

I can't explain why I don't make my epic sauntering walk away from him. I can't. I'm frozen in place beneath the weight of his now urgent features. He seems torn between begging and screaming for me to listen to him. It's a magnetic feeling between us to see him caught in the emotions I've felt all day.

His head shakes slowly, and it seems methodical the way he pushes his hands down his thighs, takes a deep inhale, and looks back up at me.

"Someday, you'll regret the choices you didn't make, Cersia."

A shiver races across my flesh at the sound of my name spoken so heartbreakingly sad against his lips.

You'll regret the choices you didn't make...

What does that mean?

You'll never know, my beast whispers.

Unknown panic shoves into my chest so suddenly it steals my breath and consumes my heart. Fear is a painful, stabbing vengeance on my soul.

It's all I know as I watch him walk away. His lazy steps lead him out to the tree line I first spotted him at. It's like the moon follows that beautiful, infuriating man as he leaves me.

He leaves me to the fate I didn't choose.

He leaves me to the life I don't want.

He just simply leaves me.

But I can't seem to let him go.

The window is pushed up once more. My feet tangle in my dress as I leap from the room. The sound of fabric tearing rips through the night air. That beautiful mating gown is ruined in the matter of one single reckless second.

And I couldn't give one fuck less about it as I follow after a new fate.

THREE

THE PLOT

I KEEP the distance between us even as my bare feet meet the sharp points of nature. Leaves and twigs scatter beneath my steps, and I know he knows I'm here. He's just too annoyingly cocky to glance back at the woman following him desperately into the shadows.

On the surface, it doesn't seem like a brilliant idea. And if he were a stronger, larger, possibly more intimidating male, I might think twice about it.

But I know I'm more capable than the cock cuddler ahead of me.

I'm not the least bit worried. Not at all.

Until the dark trees around us fall away, and two other men stand in a clearing beneath the full light of my Goddess Moon.

Fuck...

I pause there at the lining of the trees. A hundred yards separate me from my pack. No one knows I'm here.

And now I am outnumbered.

But I am fierce.

My spine straightens. When all three of them look up at me, that familiar look of surprised awe touches their brows. It's a look I normally roll my eyes at, but right now I'm more concerned about whether they think they just hit the homicide jackpot.

I take a single step back, and at the same time, one of them takes a slow cautious step forward. "We don't want to hurt you," he says in a voice of sensual serenity. The sound of it is like a warm breeze caressing my skin.

"I mean, we can't guarantee she won't be, either," The Hell Cunt who brought me here scoffs with a deadly smile nicking his lips.

"Roman," the larger man in the middle warns, speaking for the first time.

His pure black hair is pulled back, and the length of it is tethered tightly against the back of his head, but several braids are strung throughout it. It's the one thing I notice. The other man also has a thick braid tying his hair back to a bun at the back of his head.

All except for Hell Cunt Roman. His is shaved close.

No pretty updos for him, it seems.

The three of them don't wear a stitch of clothing, and every line of their hard bodies is painted in the moonlight.

I assess the level of threat their strength implies... Sure, I also assess other uses for their toned, perfect bodies, but the girth and length of certain parts of them go nearly unnoticed.

...*Nearly*.

"My mate will come looking for me," I tell them calmly with a casual tilt of my chin. "He's the jealous type. Very hostile. And when he shifts, I can't stop the violence of his beast."

Lies. Lies. Lies.

If Mika were the jealous type, he wouldn't mate with the one woman every male in this pack leers at from afar.

"Mate?" Hell Cunt whispers, looking to the guy who seems very much in charge of the burly band of idiots.

"She has no mate." The caressingly peaceful voice of the appraising shifter is the calmer man of the three and he dares to take another slow step closer. "Her words were spoken too quickly. She's afraid of us. You don't have to be afraid of us," he reassures once more, and my ovaries would honestly believe any sweet fucking word he said as long as he keeps talking like he's a breath away from an orgasm. His tone is too poetic. Too calming.

It's too sweet right now when my mind is racing between trusting him and killing him. He's a watchful man. Except he doesn't actually watch me. He assesses the air around where I stand, and he has yet to meet my peering eyes.

It's...odd...very—

"Are you blind?" I blurt suddenly as the interest in me becomes too much.

"I am." As he confirms it, a shy smile presses to his

full lips, and I don't know why the simple fact makes me trust him even more.

He can't see me. He has no idea if I'm the most beautiful woman in the world or an ass goblin looking for a new hole to crawl into. It's exhilarating.

"She's not nearly as pretty as the Night Witch babbled," Hell Cunt tells his blind friend.

And though I appreciate that the blind man can't judge me on my appearance, I'm fucking outraged that this asshole continuously ignores the fact that he'd give his right nut for the chance to inhale my breath during flu season.

There he goes again, wrecking my humbleness.

I release a very quiet, very composed sigh as I meet this gaze.

He fucking smiles.

My middle finger twitches.

While I glare so hard my eyes hurt, the largest of the three men stomps forward. His weight breaks the sticks and twigs beneath his bare feet with so much force it seems impossible he's just simply walking instead of violently battling nature itself.

When he's close enough, his big hand comes out and snatches up my jaw. My nails embed into his wrist in the span of a sharp inhale within my throat, and we hold each other in a way that might seem intimate to the naked eye.

Except my jaw hurts, and his flesh beneath my nails is bleeding down his forearm.

Very, very intimate.

He has eyes so pale they're more white than green. But those bursts of lime are there in his hard gaze as he appraises every little curve of my face. It's like he's trying to understand me, trying to read me. I feel the press of his attention. It heats my cheeks, but I refuse to do anything more than glare up at the savage man.

"She'll do," he grunts before flinging my face away and stalking back the way he came.

"What the fuck is with you cock knots?" The words spew out before I can stop them.

"Cock knots?" The gentler man repeats with a curl of his lips like he can physically taste those words and they do not appear to taste good.

How do they not get it?

No!

No, I won't *do*. I'm not a pig being prepared for the slaughter. I am the most beautifully blessed woman in all the land, and I deserve more communication than manhandling gropes and Neanderthal grunts.

My arm flies out, and the feel of soft, long locks are twisted through my fingers before he even makes it two steps. His balance wavers, but instead of falling, he simply follows the motion of my hand, arching his back severely until he's looking up at me from an upside-down angle.

"I'm going to ask you very, very calmly to release my hair." The shadowy scruff along his jaw shifts as though his teeth are grinding with every word he says.

"Never touch a High Hell's braids," someone says in a hushed warning.

I disregard both of their comments. "Tell me what you three want from me." The tension in my arm is taut. I'm ready.

He's ready.

And yet, neither of us move.

"Rome didn't tell you?" he barks, keeping his posture in a nearly perfect backbend while losing his composure in his growling tone. "Rome!"

"It didn't come up," the asshole with the cruel smirk says.

The kinder man at his side peers over at Rome with disappointment and annoyance in his gaze. It seems in this moment, we all think little Romey is a cock dangler.

The large man settled against my palm closes his eyes as a long and tiring sigh slips from his full lips. A thin scar kisses his mouth along his lower lip, fading into the shining black hair of his beard. Bronze skin is smooth and flawless against hard features.

He's brutally handsome. So distractingly so, that my fingers loosen their hold, and before I can stop myself, I stroke my palm through his soft hair.

Every strand slides through my long fingers like the finest satin.

Green eyes open so fast that I flinch. Not from fear though. From being caught acting so outrageously stupid.

What is wrong with me?

And why is his hair so well-conditioned? He isn't a wolf at all but a prized show dog fresh from the groomer.

He blinks away the confusion in his gaze, and now that I'm all but stroking his mane instead of threatening his life, he gradually corrects his stance. He takes his time turning toward me, and I can see the uncomfortable look still lingering in his eyes.

Thankfully he seems to ignore the mishap.

Thank the Goddess.

"My name's Zilo. That's Roman." He points to my dearest fuck-hole friend, and Romey doesn't so much as nod my way. "And the one who actually knows how to talk to women is Avian." Avian's blind gaze stares straight ahead, but an alluring mixture of a smile like kindness and sex pulls at his lips as he waves softly.

I don't tell them my name. They already know it. Instead, I cling harder to the aggression in my gaze as my arms fold over my chest and I stare up at the enormous man.

Goddess, he's like a small mountain. I've never been much of an adventurist before, but I suddenly have the urge to climb new heights.

"What is it you want from me, Zilo?" I can't help the way my tongue accentuates his name.

It isn't sexy. Why am I making it sexy?

"We're warriors of hell."

Interesting. The High Hell are warriors. Impressive.

"Annnd," I drawl as if none of this is the most enthralling thing to ever happen in my meager little life.

"Our ruler is Ravar, Prince of Hell."

Goddess, it's like I've stepped foot into a novel. Too bad this asshole has the poorest pacing I've ever heard.

Get. To. The. Plot. For Goddess sake, Zilo. You're as pretty as you are dull.

"We...we wish to get rid of the Prince of Hell."

My eyes widen, and I can't contain the anxious, excited thrumming inside me.

"You want me to help you overthrow your ruler?" My brows arch, but they cut even higher when Romey speaks up.

"*Kill.* Actually. We want to kill the fucker."

"That's treason. If you could please watch your tongue." Avian swipes his blind attention toward the man at his side, but Rome appears unthreatened by the warning as he gives a long and slow eye roll.

"We don't want you to lift a finger against anyone. We simply want..." Zilo's deep voice drowns off slightly before picking back up. "We need an insider. A beautiful distracting insider."

The plot thickens.

"And why do you think the Prince of Hell would have any interest in me?"

"Because it's the ten-thousandth year of his reign. Every one thousand years, he seeks out a new bride to bless him with her attention."

"Wait just one fucking minute. You want me to marry the Prince of Hell?" My tone balances shakily on a shriek.

"No, just seduce him. Marriage isn't necessary yet."

"*Yet?*" There it is. There's the shriek.

A tumbling laugh skims from Rome's lips, and my glare slides to him.

I'm stunned how fast the look shuts him up.

Maybe he does have a few ounces of intelligence rattling around in that obnoxiously pretty head of his.

There's a tense seriousness on each of their faces. No. Not seriousness. Desperation. I guarantee they'd never admit it, but they're desperate. They want change for some reason.

And they want me specifically to be on their side.

"You're an outsider," Avian explains. "You have no loyalty to the kingdom of hell unlike the women in our realm. We want your loyalty."

They're smart. They've thought this through.

"Doesn't hurt that she's fucking beautiful." Rome surprises me with that comment, and though it's spoken like a harsh insult it warms me in a way.

I knew it. I knew he thought I was pretty.

The pretentious fucker.

"So...I put my life in literal hellacious danger to traitorously feed you the son of Satan's secrets...and you give me..." A dramatic pause lingers for so long the three idiots finally pick up on insinuation.

"Oh, uh, I don't know. A way out of your shitty life? How about that?" Rome spits those words at me, and Avian turns on him. In under half a second, his fist is thrust into Rome's gut, and the Hell Cunt doubles over with a satisfying grunt.

"She's a lady. Speak to her as such," Avian growls, his arm still flexed hard. Meanwhile, my panties have never been wetter. *He's adorably sweet and protectively aggressive?* Is there anything more a high-class *lady* such as myself could ever ask for?

"My life isn't shitty." My chin lifts high with all the pride a shifter like myself will always hold. And maybe a little higher because that's just how much confidence I've been raised to carry.

"It ain't pretty though, is it, beautiful?" Roman's words are like a stab to the chest, and the pain that I feel there is all-consuming.

Because he's right.

I don't want the path I'm following.

I've known these guys for all of ten minutes, and the challenge they're offering me is exactly what my father trained me for. I'm meant for battle and adventure. Danger and mystery.

I just want—I want more.

My arms lower casually to my sides. I relax my shoulders, my spine and my neck. They watch me in apprehensive silence. They know too much about me. They've done their homework and they seem to know what I'm capable of and what I want and don't want in life.

They know I don't want what have. Why does it sting to realize they seem to know that more than even I do.

I... I want a life they're trying to give me.

A slow sigh crawls up my throat and it feels like a weight is pulled right off of me with the simple exhale and acceptance of it all.

"Lead the way, boys," I whisper with the smallest smile touching my lips.

All three of them look as stunned as I feel in this moment.

Zilo lifts his big hand and gestures to the vagueness of the dark night set out ahead of us.

And then I follow these three beautiful strangers into the unknown.

But will they still want me when they know all of my secrets...

FOUR

THE KINGDOM OF HELL

"Is there a hell hole somewhere? A pit? A handbasket perhaps?" I've trailed along in silence for so long I just can't take it anymore, and the word vomit spews from my lips with all the things I've been thinking for at least an hour.

The attractive lines of Zilo's muscular back deepen, and he turns to me with a disturbed glare in his pale green eyes.

"What the f—what are you talking about a basket?" he growls.

"*Hell*. How will we be getting to hell?" I blink at him, but it's Romey who makes the first comment. Or sneer, I should say.

"You think you get to hell in a handbasket? You're a fucking beautiful mess, aren't you?" That carving smile of his is nasty in a way. Cruelty stings his words like that smirk kisses his lips. Even if he says the most lovely thing, it's stained in abuse. I don't know what hurt him, but he seems adamant to return the favor to every single person who so much as looks his way.

"Once we're far enough away from all civilization, I'll be our maker," Avian explains, not noticing Rome's dark demeanor one bit. I know he's blind, but...he must feel it right? Does he know how much his friend hurts?

Do any of them even remotely care about each other in that way? Or is the plan to overthrow a ruler just a job to them, just as High Hell is a job to them? Are their relationships a job to them?

"Maker?" I ignore all their flaws among one another and try to understand.

"The magic of hell is fueled by the realm itself. Men like Roman and Zilo, they're impossibly strong within the realm of hell. But I'm a maker. I can carry that magic with me. I'll make our entryway for us. It'll be safe and easy. You do not have to worry." His hand lifts toward me, but he doesn't touch. He's polite and sensitive.

How the hell did Avian end up with these two obtuse alpha-holes? They have the emotional capacity of a burnt hotdog. The personality to match too.

"Just do it here. I haven't heard a single footstep in miles." Roman's serious for once. A thin line of concern is against his dark eyebrows. And stranger than that, his long fingers touch Avian's upper arm in a comforting way I didn't even realize he was capable of.

It's then that the light of the moon brightens the

white lines that cut across Roman's back. They're jagged and harsh. Deeper in some places and longer in others.

They're scars.

My stomach jolts at the sight of the viciousness marring his golden skin. My insides crumble, but the men don't give me time to process the thousands of wounds this man carries with him every day.

"If I'm caught, they'll singe my magic," Avian whispers, his silver eyes big with concern as he looks up at the man at his side.

I want to look away when Rome's thumb brushes back and forth along the smooth, sun-kissed skin of Avian's lined bicep. I want to. But I don't.

Roman doesn't reassure his friend. He doesn't seem to be the type to understand or offer that kind of comfort.

But he does keep his fingers gentle against Avian. It's the smallest connection. It's an unspoken passing of comradery.

And it seems to be all that the maker needs.

For he lifts his index finger just above his head. It sparks with golden and charcoal colors that burn into the night air. He cascades his magic down in one long swooping line that turns to fire right before my very eyes.

Within a matter of seconds, a perfect circle is burning in glittering sunbursts like a tunnel into the depths of pure shadows and emptiness. It's nothing short of incredible artisan magic.

"To enter, I'll have to lower our wards, and you'll have to be in your true form." Avian turns to me, and my heart dead falls right into the deepest part of my turning stomach.

"I-I can't do that." I shake my head so fast my pale blonde locks shift along my face.

"What?" Zilo's rumbling tone is hinting at aggression as it seems to always be doing.

It isn't fucking helping right now.

"Shift. Every second of our time that you waste is another chance for Avian's magic to be spotted. Fucking change. Now!" Roman takes a hard pounding step into my space, and my nails bite into my palm at his storming closeness.

"Calm down, Rome," Avian warns.

"Listen to your friend," I whisper through clenched teeth.

Roman's thick eyebrows lift high, and I can physically feel his power radiating off his smooth chest. It's a spark in his eyes. He wants the altercation. It's something that gives him life. Maybe that's all he has.

But right now is not the time.

"I physically can't shift," I say as rationally and steadily as I can.

"You can't or *won't*?" Zilo tilts his head low, and though he isn't as forceful as his friend here, I know he's just as powerful. More powerful from the looks of him.

"I can't. I try and I feel it build but just...never happens." I swallow hard at the self-conscious confession that I've kept secret from everyone I've ever met.

It's my secret. And I just gave it away to three strangers for the simple price of early admission into hell.

"Ah, so it's performance anxiety, huh?" Rome's perfectly snarling smirk is right back against his lips.

"I fucking hate you," I finally tell him.

"I know." He leans into me. His warm words wash over my neck as he whispers once more. "Feels good, doesn't it?"

My palms collide hard into his chest, his warm skin lingering along my fingertips for what feels like an eternity. Especially when he grips my wrists and pulls me forcefully against his nakedness.

The slamming of my heart kicks in just as I lift my leg, my knee grazing against the spot just between his thighs. His eyes widen with sparking interest. Excitement. Deranged insanity.

But my knee never connects.

And his pain never seems to come.

Because with the next pounding of my heart, heat floods my flesh. It scorches my skin. It fucking drowns me in pain.

Smoke and fire blaze in slashing colors, but I fade away into nothingness before I can fully see the effects of my surroundings.

And then...I'm pacing on four strong, powerful legs.

What. The. Fuck.

First time, huh, beautiful? An annoying little voice says at the back of my mind. *Avian would have taken things slow with you, but it feels better when it's fast and hard, doesn't it?*

The forest is a blur of dense darkness around me. When I try to speak, a pathetic little whine is all that comes out.

No one likes a whiner. Stop. You're making us look bad. Roman's voice is all I know.

I can hear him. I can feel him.

"You didn't have to absorb her," Avian scolds.

When my—Roman's—head looks up, Avian is staring down at us. A familiar look of disappointment is in his boyish features.

"Whatever. We need to go," Zilo says and then, in an explosion of smoke, he too shifts. An enormous beast with shining black fur and jagged white teeth now stands at my side.

Without a second wasted, he leaps paws first through the fiery circle of golden magic.

A long drawn out sigh shoves from Avian's lips as he shakes his head. Another pulse of fireworks and a lean, chestnut brown wolf stands where the sweet man just was.

You'll be okay. Avian's smooth voice whispers through my head, just a bit more distant than Roman's had. It's like glass separates him and me. *We'll take care of you. We won't let anyone harm you.*

It's a calming sentiment.

Too bad Roman doesn't let it last. *He literally cannot*

promise you that. You'll be lucky if you make it one day in this hell hole of a kingdom.

I fucking hate you, I whisper like a caress.

I know, he says right back.

With me in tow, he leaps. My heart free-falls as we descend into the warming feel of consuming magic.

And if I could have kicked that fur fucker in the balls just one second earlier, I would have.

When we shakily land in the depths of new darkness, I feel hands wrapped around my lower back. I can't explain it as I stand on four furry legs, and yet, I'm held intimately against a strong protecting male.

Sorry, someone says within my mind in a gravelly, quiet tone. So quiet that I don't immediately recognize it as Roman's voice at all.

He's awkward in this moment as the hold slips away with lingering fingertips against the skin I no longer see but still completely feel.

It's—it's whatever. Not a big deal, I tell him.

If I could cough out an uncomfortable sigh in this moment, I would.

Why is my heart pounding so hard?

Because you're in hell, maybe? he answers my rambling in that cruel careless way I'd expect from him.

That's better.

Our wolf shakes out its head, and we gaze around at

the shadows. I see nothing, but I sense the two other wolves standing at our side. They're silent, but in their silence, I feel more at ease from their nearness. Their power feels like my power. Their confidence is my own. And their comradery is something that surges in my heart like pumping blood rushing right through my veins.

This must be what it feels like to truly be a part of a pack.

I've never felt it in my entire life, but it feels so damn comforting it burns my eyes with wetness and causes my beast to release a long drawn out whine.

Stopppp. You're making us look like pussies, Romey scolds.

My snark is right on the tip of my tongue, but the words crawl right back down my throat and hide in fear when a crisp white face snaps into color among the blackness.

What. The. Unholy. Fuck.

"Who's your friend, boys?" The bone white face asks, her lips the color of ebony and her teeth rotting among the darkness of her tongue.

"Creatchin, I see you're taking advantage of the wards being down." Zilo pauses for only a second, and when she doesn't answer, he continues. "This is Lady Cersia." Zilo's proud booming voice echoes loudly in my head, making me flinch immediately.

But the woman seems to hear him.

I don't know how, but she does.

"Mmm, yes. The beautifully pained woman. Beautifully pained indeed." With a single step, her willowy figure bursts from the shadows. Spindly arms and long fingers like spider's legs reach out for my beast as well as myself.

And I have to force my confidence and not back away from her ice-cold touch along my head, my pointed ears, and the long curve of my thick neck.

"She'll do just fine. He'll absolutely devour her." Her big black eyes eat me whole as I simply stare up at her from my low place on the ground. "Make sure you train her. She's harboring many secrets, that one. We do not have time for another dead bride." With a turn of her lips and a terrifying smile, she vanishes.

And I'm left gaping at that last line that hangs like a noose in the dark.

Dead bride? I scream the word so loud all three of them, my own wolf included, cower and whine, crawling around the shadows like scattering mice.

There was an...incident last week, Avian answers.

He has the balls to answer but the intelligence to be vague.

An incident that included a dead bride.

And now they want me to be the next in line to fill that vacancy.

Fucking cowards.

All of them.

Enough, Roman roars.

The smoke that shatters around me slices my skin in a strange abrasive way. But worse than that...I'm wet, I'm drenched from head to toe when my bare feet meet the smooth concrete.

My fingers stick to one another, thick goop sliding down my skin in a gagging sensation that makes me do just that.

I turn this way and that before bumping into a hard shoulder that is just so arrogant I know it's him.

"What—what am I covered in?" I stare up at the space where I imagine those cruel condescending eyes to be.

A huff of a laugh shakes out of him and fans along my disgustingly damp cheek. Steady fingertips push back my slick hair, and when it tucks behind my ear, it's pure nasty stickiness.

Please don't be cum. Please don't be cum. Please don't be cum.

"My mucus, beautiful."

My throat constricts with a heaving I can't repress. It shoves against my chest with every gag I cough out.

"Oh. My. Fucking. Goddess." My stomach lurches once more, but even in my sickness, I still can't help the anger that rises above it all.

My nails dig into hard shoulders, and I bring him down in one swift turn kick. But I don't let him go that easily. I'm on top of him in a flash of speed. My knuckles are so covered in his fucking bodily fluid that the punches slap right off the hard edges of his face.

I can't see him.

But I hear his discomfort. And that's all that motivates me to keep going. With every grunting groan, I slam my fist down all over again.

Again.

And again.

And again.

Until several hands grab my hips.

I'm hauled off of him. My back collides with smooth skin, and those strong hands continue to hold me in place against his chest. Even if I'm not struggling to fuck up that pretty face any longer.

I feel good. It feels good to finally release all the rage I've been pushing down within myself for so damn long.

It's freeing.

It's ecstasy.

Until Rome laughs. An amusement tinged with breathless pain kisses the darkness, and he just—why does he piss me off without saying a Goddessdamn word?!

"You're cute when you're murderous, beautiful," the Hell Cunt grunts as he stands, his warmth coming close enough to infuriate me all over again.

Only when I stop trembling with fury do the arms around me slowly slide down my arms, my wrists, ever so gently over my tightly held fists. It's like he steals away my anger with that hypnotic touch that shivers down deep into my core.

I just know it's Avian. It's his calming caress.

It's distracting.

For a moment.

My fist is balled up once more and flung forward immediately the moment I'm free from Avian's calming hold. My punch is straightforward and cracking against the smooth line of Roman's nose.

A growl is followed closely by excessive curses that bring a pleased smile to my lips.

"Fuck! Are you just irrationally violent all of the time?" Hell Cunt asks on a muffled grunt.

"That's enough. Stop antagonizing her," a deep voice commands.

"Me? What about her?" Romey's all but pouting while I'm all but sticking my tongue out at the fucker in victory.

Mom likes me best. Get over it, Bro.

"Avian, come with me to check in with the Prince. Someone will be suspicious if the High Hell don't report tonight." Zilo's orders seem endless and articulate. Even I'm nodding along like I have a clue what's happening at the moment. "Rome, take the girl to our bedroom. Don't let her out, and don't let her be seen. And for hell's sake, fix your fucking nose. It's disgusting." Strong and direct footfalls stride away from me, and I'm left stunned in the dark.

With Roman.

His hand wraps around my upper arm with just enough tightness to tell me he's still pissed about the bloody nose thing.

I can't see where we're going. The flooring is cold concrete. It's not dirty but not perfectly even either. A slight chill bites the air, and I can't help but wonder why the temperature is so low for hell. I imagined it a bit more...stuffy, I suppose.

Roman jerks me around this way and that as we turn maze-like corners every few steps we take, and he has yet to speak to me.

Perhaps I should apologize.

Perhaps I should not.

Definitely the latter. Yes. Definitely not.

My shoulders square despite how often my feet want to stumble. I don't, of course. I keep up, and I let him brood the entire way. He stops us so abruptly that my mucus-sticky chest collides into his smooth shoulder. He tenses. I wait. I count the beats of my heart, and three pulses slip by in the awkward silence before the churn of metal turning with a quiet click sounds just lightly.

And pale light casts across his golden skin.

With one strong pull and shove, he tosses me onto a bed. The springs bounce beneath me, and my anger wants to rise up all over again, but I swallow it down and peer around at my new surroundings instead. I take an inventory of every detail.

I do a fine job indeed of pretending to ignore the naked brooding man in the room.

No windows line the tall black brick walls. The stone shimmers like beautiful poison glimmering among so much ebony. A black velvet settee faces a cold empty fire pit in the middle of the room. Two Victorian-style chairs also surround the circular pit, though they appear to be carved from black onyx, with sharp pointed backs.

Every inch of the room, including the bed I sit on, is inky or at best, dark ash. The sheets are silk beneath my touch. The color of charred coal. And the bed: it's fucking enormous. A dozen wolves could sleep in this thing and never once so much as brush up against the other.

"Whose room is this?" My lashes lift, and I find Roman hunched over a basin bowl in the corner, his features darker than usual as he wipes away dried blood from the bruising bridge of his nose.

Ouch.

...No. Still not sorry.

With the crimson-soaked cloth, he dabs once more, his eyes closing, his shoulders bunching together so tightly a line etches down the hard muscles of his shoulder blades.

Do not help him, Cersia. Do not pity him. He's a cruel, cruel man. Do not extend kindness to the cruel, for they will accept it and then step on it until it bends, until it bows and until it finally breaks.

Roman is the type of man who could break me. His sea like eyes are too pained. He's too handsome and too hurt to know how to be gentle with a crumpled heart like mine.

So I seal up the cage that surrounds the little beating thing in my chest.

And then I look away from the blood on his face.

"It's the High Hell's bedroom. We're the final three of our realm." I can hear the disdain in his voice.

He fucking hates me.

Good.

It's mutual.

"The three of you share a room?" *And more importantly a bed?*

I can't help but remember the way he briefly showed Avian a different side of him. A softer side. A fleetingly fragile side of himself.

"We share everything. We'll share a life, and we'll share our enemies. We'll do anything to protect the last of our kind. We're the tormented. We're the surviving. We're the darkest wolves hell has ever created..." His words slip away into a heavy breath that keeps his full lips parted as he seems to think about his bond he shares with Zilo and Avian.

"Hell created you?" I arch a brow at him, my fingers steadily pushing back my crisp and dry blonde hair to really appraise the lean physique of the man still turned away from me. Hard lines are all he's made of. They slash across his ribs and clatter down his torso, his hips, his thighs. His arms and even his lower back are sliced in pure violent strength.

I just can't bring myself to think about his scars.

"The Prince of Hell made us. He makes all of us. We fight for him and his realm. We honor his name as tormentor and ruler of lands."

"How does he make you?" The words fall from my

lips as my mind flashes with too many images of what he could possibly be meaning.

Roman turns then, his hands bracing against the black tabletop behind him as he looks at me through slitted eyes and dark lined lashes. "He instills unyielding fight into our blood. He blesses us with unimaginable ruthlessness."

"You mean *cruelty*," I correct. But he ignores the statement.

"And he does it by showing us first-hand how it feels. Every day of our lives. Until we no longer cry to be saved. When our whimpers fade and our heads still rise to face his punishment, that's when he knows we're ready to carry his name across realms and lands. He makes us, Cersia. And soon, he'll make you his bride." That smile cuts across beautiful features in a haunting look of asinine pleasure.

A chill scratches across my flesh, and I can't break his gaze. I couldn't look away from this demented psycho if I wanted to.

I left a man who would protect me for a man who will hurt me. And I did it without thinking twice.

Why? Why am I so blind when it comes to love? Mika loved me! He did.

I just didn't deserve it. I deserve war. I deserve this.

And that's why I'm here.

My spine straightens, and I sit up in the massive bed. "I can take it," I say with nothing but confidence.

One of his eyebrows arches in an adorable way that I can't ignore.

"Really?" With force, he shoves off from his leaning spot across the room, and he prowls toward me, one foot in front of the other, with perfect predatorial pride. When he's near enough, his knee lifts and he props himself there at the foot of the bed. A safe space of four feet separates me from the arrogant Hell Cunt whose nose I've already bloodied once tonight.

Does he want to clean up his pretty boy face all over again?

Every move he makes is accounted for. I glare at him hard, but I note every single ticking muscle that tenses beneath that golden skin of his. His palms flatten against the smooth black blanket. One by one, his fingers dig in, fisting the fine cloth into his palms.

And then he pounces.

He shoves off from his perch so fast I don't process it at all. It's a blur of movement. And a slamming of hard body weight forces me down beneath him.

"You can take it?" he growls as his nails dig into my wrists above my head.

Power radiates off of him in heated waves, but I never move. I let him show me everything he's harboring. Every inch of his body aligns with mine, his hips hard between my thighs as his lips graze along my jawline.

And still I do nothing but watch him.

And wait.

And wait.

And wait.

Confusion lines his brow, and he searches my face.

He embarrassed me, covered me in his mucus, and now he forces me down to show me who's in charge.

I see the role here. I do. And I know exactly what the point is he's trying to make.

Will I break in this kingdom of hell?

"Where's your fucking fight now?" He jerks against my wrists harder, stretching me out even more beneath him. I don't so much as shift against his dominating frame. "Fight, Cersia!" he commands, but it isn't like Zilo. It isn't the sound of dominance.

It's the sound of desperation.

How did his prince break him so hard for his tortured soul to be so hellbent on hurting everyone he meets?

"No," I whisper so softly it hurts to say the simple word to him.

Why do I have this reaction to him? Why do I have the sudden illogical urge to wrap my arms around him and never let anything in this world hurt him?

"You have to fight here." Big jewel-like eyes are soft as he studies the curves of my features. "If you don't fight—"

"They'll break me," I finish for him. Strong hands slip off of mine, and I catch his fingers in mine before he has a chance to slip away. I hold his hands the same way he was just holding me. But not to force violence from him. I do it to ensure he knows I'm here. I'm here because of him. *For* him...

"They'll break me either way, Roman. How I react to

their torment is what will earn me insight into who they are. And what their weaknesses are." At that, he suddenly seems aware of how intimately he's pressed against me. My fingers are intertwined with his, our chests are melded perfectly together, and...and his cock is very hard against my center.

Who would have thought kindness was this bastard's weakness?

His long fingers fling out, and he pulls his hands as well as every single part of him swiftly away from me. He's striding across the room in less than half a second.

It's my turn to smile smugly.

"You need to get changed. Clean up. You look disgusting." He lifts a hand, gesturing toward a bathtub in the corner, and I note there are several ivory gowns hanging on a hook just to the left of the shining black tub.

For the next several minutes, he does a fine job pretending his thick cock isn't still jutting out as he pulls out a pair of black jeans and starts carelessly pulling them on.

While I watch him like he's my new favorite hobby.

I will understand him. I will learn everything about him. And then...yeah, then I might do him.

Because that's what hobbies are for, filling the hole in our life and such.

A frustrated sigh parts my lips, and I mimic him as I too pretend he isn't just a few yards from me while I consider the massive bath filling the corner with strange but mesmerizing glittering black water practically inviting me in. It all feels sort of unreal in a way.

The last twenty-four hours are a chaotic mess in my mind.

I really changed my life.

I might actually change theirs...

I shake the thoughts away as I pull the string of the gown at the base of my neck and let the thin material fall away. Cold air bites at my skin, but the steam of the bathwater licks at my flesh invitingly when I step in.

When I look up, deep eyes lock with mine. Only a second does he hold my gaze. Because then his attention falls. He traces the curves of my body with big, hungry attention that I feel against my flesh. I can physically feel his gaze brushing along my shoulders, my breasts, my stomach, my—

"I didn't leer at your cock when you were naked." My hands meet my hips hard, and I tilt my head at him accusingly.

"The fuck you didn't. You looked, measured, and scrapbooked my cock the first moment we met."

My lips part with outrage, but I can usually conceal my smile with years of practiced articulate anger. But a small smile creases my features anyway. Maybe I did have a peek...or two...or nine. Inches...

What were we talking about?

There's a heated moment, like the flint of spark just before the blaze, where we're both staring at one another with something other than hate in our eyes as I sink all the way down into the bath. My head dips below the enchanting waters, and it rejuvenates me in an electric way before I slip back to the surface.

I lift my hand to find every speck of dirt washed away and my skin glowing with a warm touch of magic that I don't understand in the slightest. The water isn't heavily fumed with a rose or lilac scent but it cleans me perfectly all the same.

The intensity of Roman's stare is now alight with a near smirk. His heavy gaze drops down to the inky line of water drifting against my chest, just above the slick curve of my breasts. I feel that look everywhere across my flesh and especially just between my now shifting thighs.

And then...and then the fucking door opens with a jarring slam that rattles the pale chandelier light above the bed.

The moment's lost. Along with any emotion I might have been stupid enough to imagine that man possessed for me.

"Punishment," a familiar commanding voice growls.

My chin flings up immediately, and there stands all six foot several inches of Zilo. His brow is hard and lowered over those alluring angry eyes of his. He appears monstrous now. He was massive in height before, but something about the fury in his features turns his size into a creature of impossible stature.

"The Prince says an exiled woman entered the kingdom. *Again*." Zilo lingers on that word before continuing. "To teach you to better guard his realm, you're to be punished... *Again.*" Once more, that word stings the man's throat, but he clears it hard and carries on. "On your knees." He stares head on at Roman, neither of them blinking as I try to process this new bizarre form of alpha'ry. The door closes with a quiet click, and Avian lingers there with several feet separating him from the other two High Hell.

"Again?" Rome says in a lifeless tone that jolts fear into my chest. It's like I can feel him right now.

And fear is not something I knew he had inside him until this very moment.

"Your Prince commanded it." Zilo's jaw clenches hard, his dark five o'clock shadow jumping with the regret that's lining his face.

Roman drops to his knees, bows his head before his friend, and accepts whatever's next.

"What—" I nearly get the question out, but it halts on my tongue the second a fiery lined whip lashes out from Zilo's fist. It snaps across the flesh of Roman's back with a sizzling cry, and my own soundless cry follows. But I can't stay silent for long.

I never can.

"Stop it!" I'm leaping from the bath and sliding over the glossy black floorboards before the man even has time to bring the strange flaming whip back for another round. My arms fling out, exposing every inch of myself to him, and I don't give one fuck what he sees in me. Beauty and lunacy go hand in hand, and I'm a displayed image of that. "Don't you fucking touch him."

Wet, pale hair hangs in my eyes, but it doesn't disrupt my glare or my seriousness.

Zilo searches my face.

Only for a fraction of a second though. "*Move*," he growls out in a gravelly tone of violence.

"Move, Cersia," Avian whispers in agreement.

I don't peer back at the man on the ground behind me, but I can just sense the irrational mutt nodding along with his besties like a happy little triad of stupidity.

"If three lashes of the Weak Whip aren't used, the Prince will know. And it will be much worse, I promise. So just walk on over to Avian, put your pretty blonde head in his chest, and don't look back, beautiful," Roman instructs, as if he's giving a meeting agenda.

My hands fall to my side from the mere sound of his defeated voice.

That's it? He just...he fucking takes it? This is what their life is here? This Prince takes friends and makes them abusers? And everyone's just supposed to accept it?

That's why I'm here.

That doesn't mean I can just leave him though. Who the hell just walks away when someone broken is being shattered?

My attention slips to the red-hot whip blazing in Zilo's fist. He too looks frantic beyond repair. It's clear he doesn't want to watch his friend be tormented either. Much less be the tormentor.

For now, he doesn't have a choice.

None of us do.

It never crosses my mind to do as Roman told me. I can't turn away from him.

And so I don't.

My legs slowly give out, and in all my glorious nudity, I wrap my arms around him chest to chest. His body is hot against mine. His heartbeat is a slamming, furious thing along my cold flesh. He stiffens against my touch. Several moments pass as I nuzzle my face into the warm crook of his neck, and only when I breathe in the scent of his fear do his rough, calloused hands skim down my slick ribs. It's the slowest caress that shakes through my soul. It skitters across my body in waves of teasing adrenaline. Until his fingers stop just at the small of my back, and he holds me hard against him, bracing himself for what's about to come.

I hear the arch of the whip before his body jolts against mine. I flinch from the whisking sound of it, and dampness stings my tightly closed eyes when a low growl of agony stifles against Roman's lips.

He holds me harder. His arms tense around me so tightly he trembles.

Something akin to a desperate, anguished kiss brushes along the side of my throat. The sound of his pain hums over the side of my neck as he buries his head in my hair, and I just hold onto him like I'll never let him go.

I'll never let him suffer alone.

I will never let that motherfucker get away with this.

I refuse.

The third and final lash of the whip comes down, licking my fingers with the feel of hot stabbing pain, washing over me in a muted agony of what this strong and beautiful man is feeling.

What he's been feeling for probably all his life.

And I vow, Prince Ravar will die for what he's done to these men.

FIVE
PUPPY TRAINING

When I wake the next morning, I find myself in a similar position as before; I'm still clinging to Roman's hard chest, and he's still holding me like I'm the only thing in the world keeping him together. His breathing is no longer frantic like it was then. His heartbeat is a mellow sound that's soothing to feel so near to my own.

I don't know when I curled up on the edge of the enormous black clad bed, but at some point, the three men joined me. I peek over Roman's scarred shoulder and find Zilo spread out in the middle, his biceps carved hard as he lies with his hand behind his messy black locks. His braids are scattered across the onyx silk pillow, and I can't help but recall how much they emphasized the importance of those braids... Avian lies far against the other edge of the bed, his back to me, and the middle part of his chestnut hair is still pulled back into a single braid that ends in a short knot at the back of his head.

My fingers twitch as they graze the smooth feel of Roman's short shaved hair.

No braids.

That's all I think about while my fingers trail up and down, my arms wrapped loosely around this strong but beaten man. His body is beautifully tan but nicked all over with lines of wounds now healed.

"You're startin' to be real sweet to me, beautiful," he whispers suddenly, startling me with his eyes closed and his body still completely at rest against my own. "I think I like you better when you're cursing me out."

A smile plays at my lips, and it's only then that his dark lashes lift, his gaze piercing to study me in the dimness of the light.

"I can call you a fur fucker and stroke your hair like a lover. It's called multitasking, Romey." My head cocks to the side, but I can't explain why I'm still holding him.

Or why he's still holding me. His big palm slides lower down to the small of my back as he pulls me in closer against this warm chest.

"Mmm, I'd like that even more though," he says in a low sensual tone that flutters across my neck and all through my body.

My heart is now a gooey mess that I can't control. It beats too hard, and I know he hears it. I know he knows what he's doing, and I hate it.

I hate that someone I hate can make my heart so stupid.

Like a bratty child, I pull his short hair between my finger and thumb, and he doesn't even flinch.

"What's with the braids?" I ask in a serious and not at all distracted tone.

The mischief shining in his gaze dulls like I've struck a chord. I get the feeling there are a lot of pained chords in Roman's miserable little life though.

"High Hell keep track of their battles. They wear their braids like badges to honor the lives they've taken."

The dozens of tiny braids in Zilo's hair flash through my mind. Avian has one.

Roman's hair is short and cropped close to his skull: no braids.

"You're a High Hell, but you've never been to battle?" I'm back to running my fingers over the spikey feel of his hair.

"I have," he admits in a shallow tone. It's more of a crippling exhale than a voice.

"Why don't you honor the lives you've taken then?" The moment I ask it, he releases me, pulls away and rolls over flat on his back. His lips tense with a stifled wince, and I know his wounds from last night are still fresh.

And yet, he continues to keep the space between us.

"What?" I ask with a new cautiousness in my tone.

"Just let it go, beautiful," he says as he closes his eyes like he's decided to now go back to sleep.

He's avoiding the answer. He doesn't want to tell me.

As a mature woman, I leave him in silence. It's the

adult thing to do. It's what any reasonable human would understand.

And that just doesn't sit right with me.

"Just fucking tell me. Stop being a little Hell Cunt and tell me!" I pout so hard I can feel the line crease between my eyebrows.

He turns his head ever so slowly and glares a look of pure demonic wrath my way. "Drop. It."

My lips part while my eyebrows lift slightly higher. "*Nnnnooo*," I reply in the clearest, most pronounced tone so I know his little puppy brain can understand.

Two well-thought-out blinks are his only response.

And then he's on top of me.

He pounces so fast I never see it coming until he's straddled over me, his fingers clenching my wrists above my head as he looks down on me with blazing fiery eyes. Hell is in his gaze. I feel it burning off his skin in hot waves that seep into my very bones. This kingdom's magic is alive and well in his strength now.

"Someday, you'll listen when someone speaks, beautiful," he whispers, getting in close as his nose runs the length of my jaw line.

His hands shift, and suddenly he's holding my arms higher with both wrists clenched in one big fist of his. With his free hand, he pushes my hair back and hovers his hot mouth just against the shell of my ear. I feel his breath there, and it races a shiver across every inch of my flesh.

"There are cruel, cruel men in this kingdom, beautiful. They'll break you." His voice dips, catching lightly before finding the gruffness of his tone. "I found out the hard way. I don't want you to be like me. When someone says to fucking drop it"—his words fans along my throat, and the way he holds me and the light graze of his fingers is suddenly more erotic than aggressive —"you fucking drop it." It's a warning. Not because he hates me. But because he's worried. He's worried I'll end up like him.

And I can see that in the pain of his eyes.

His grip on me loosens, and I feel him shift against my hips, the hardness beneath his pants suggesting the very heated thoughts that are flickering through my mind as well. Big dilated eyes catch mine. Our heavy breaths mingle. Our lips are so close I can taste the plea still lingering on his tongue.

A rough hand snatches my chin and tips my head up, our lips coming even more dangerously close. "Say you understand, beautiful," he whispers in a desperate tone.

I search his gaze—those beautiful light emerald eyes I remember falling into the moment he first looked at me.

He cares.

Even if he doesn't want to.

And that's why I submit. I nod to him.

There's a long moment when his attention slips down, lingering along my lips. An ache glides through me with every passing second as he realizes just how close he and I are.

It hurts to feel the tension. It hurts so good. It hurts

even more when he shoves off the mattress. He strides as far away from me as his long legs will carry him.

The door clicks closed.

He leaves.

And it's only then that I catch my breath.

Possibly for the first time since I arrived in the kingdom of hell.

"The Prince's dinner is tonight. *The* dinner," Zilo explains.

As if *the dinner* and *regular dinner* are somehow different in my mind.

Whatever. I've learned in our short twenty-four hours together that it makes those lines around his pretty eyes deepen if you interrupt him when he's plotting.

Which wouldn't be a big deal, but the motherfucker is always plotting.

Like right now for example:

"I have training with the lowers of hell this morning. Avian is going to train you for tonight. He's good. He'll make sure you're ready."

Training... Right.

I nod. Avian's soft smile is reassuring, and I feel like an idiot when I return the gesture to the blind man.

Should I be telling him when I smile? When I nod? What is the protocol here? Why am I like this?

Zilo's confidence in me wanes when he spots me

shaking my head at myself and mumbling quietly about the blonde leading the blind.

"You can do this, right?" Zilo dips his head into my line of sight. "We picked you for a reason."

"Because I'm pretty. I get it." My mouth slams together hard.

"Yes but no. Your unique beauty will get his attention. Your mouth will intrigue him—"

Avian smiles harder, and it's then that I know they have inside jokes about me.

The fur-holes.

"And it's your fighter background that will keep you alive in all this. Your inability to shift is a hazard to yourself, but you've more than made up for it in your life. You're a survivor. It isn't just your beauty, Cersia." His big hand lands on my shoulder, and I feel a tingle of pride from his words.

It's short-lived.

"So don't fuck up," he adds with total seriousness. And then he too slams the door in my face.

Nice pep talk.

"Right," I whisper to myself.

"You'll be great," Avian says smoothly.

"Great," I echo, still staring at the glossy black door.

It's a tranquil daze that skips beyond time, and I just can't snap out of it. I know I'd be more capable if I had my beast to rely on. I almost shifted once...but my father stopped me. I don't remember why, but I remember the feeling of fear.

I still feel that consuming fear every time I try to shift.

I'm lost in those thoughts. Until something very similar to a snap clicks twice in my ear. My head twitches as a shudder skims through me, and I slowly turn to the boyish man standing behind me with that same casual smile tilting his lips.

He stands shirtless, his broad chest seeming even wider in the dim candlelit lighting of the room. He's dressed in just black pants once again. Boots that lace up above his ankles give him a militia look. The men gave me similar pants and boots, but lucky me, I got an old tattered black shirt to go along with it.

In Avian's right hand, he holds a little white gadget.

His thumb presses down, and once more it clicks at me in a harsh aggravating way.

"What the fuck is that annoying little box?" My lips curl hard as I speak.

"It's a clicker trainer." He holds it out for me to observe, as if by seeing it closer I might not want to slam it to the ground and stomp on it until it no longer resembles a box at all.

"I don't get it." I eye him skeptically.

I thought when Zilo said *training*, I'd be drop-kicking Avian's sweet little attitude to the floor by now, not discussing hardware.

"Hell's kingdom is made up of many races, but hellhounds and wolves like yourself are the majority. Demons and hell fae coexist with us, but the Prince will not take disrespect. And so you need to learn his few common clicks." Avian takes a few steps closer to me, and the more he explains, the more annoyed I'm becoming.

"He clicks at hellhounds?" My left eyebrow is so high it's ready to jump ship at any moment.

"Yes." Avian nods, and a strand of his dark hair falls over his bright silver eyes.

My teeth grind, and I try so damn hard to just listen. If I just hold my tongue, surely this won't really be as demeaning as I'm imagining it.

Avian smiles.

I force a smile.

Then he ruins it all when he speaks.

"The first click we learn will be *sit*."

"Oh, for fuck's sake!"

"What? What's wrong?" Avian's hand skims my elbow lightly, and it's hard for me to not take my frustration out on him.

Roman was right: I need to listen more. I need to just listen.

I focus as I exhale ever so slowly. "Nothing." I calm myself with another breath. "I'm fine. Please continue."

Somehow I stop myself from flinging my body to the floor and kicking and screaming about the patriarchy and bigots.

I smile.

Avian smiles.

"Today we'll practice sit and silence."

My wide eyes widen impossibly more as I literally bite my cheek and smile even harder like a lunatic.

"We'll do kneel and fetch tonight after the dinner."

Kneel. Fetch. *Kneel*. And *fetch*.

What. The. Fuck.

"Nope," I blurt. "Can't do it." I'm striding to the door within half a second, and I nearly fall face first when he flashes in front of me with a spark of dark embers.

They're faster here as well as stronger. Do they even realize it?

"What are you doing?" His hands are around my shoulders, and I can't even process how powerful this man is. He could snap my bones if he really wanted to. And I don't give a single damn.

I'm too irate.

"Fetch? Are you fucking serious, Avian?!"

"You're mad," says the one man who I thought had some intelligence out of the three.

"Yes! I'm fucking mad!"

He nods like he's absorbing that info as I spew it.

"Because..." His wide eyes are empty and searching as he tries to piece together this mysterious puzzle. "Because this training is...hard?" He phrases that uncertainty in such a confused way my mouth drops wide open.

"Seriously? I'm mad because it's belittling, Av! Why the fuck would I fetch something for anyone! I've been blessed by the Goddess Moon herself!" Pain shoots through my jaw as I snap my mouth closed with force and determination. "I kneel and fetch for no one."

His palms slide down my arms so slowly it shivers across my flesh with that single touch. His dark eyebrows pull together with a look of sadness.

When he speaks, it's a heartbreaking sound. "Your Goddess means nothing in the kingdom of hell. Your ruler and master is one in the same. And if you wish to live, you'll kneel when you're told. And you'll definitely fetch whatever he wants," he whispers like it's painful to say, and I notice how slowly he takes another little step closer to me.

We're so close I have to peer up at him from beneath thick lashes. And it hurts to realize how right he is.

It hurts me. And it's easy to see that it hurts him just as much.

This powerful man before me is a slave.

And now I am too.

SIX
TOUCH ME

Two clicks sound through the room for what must be the millionth annoying time.

I seethe in silence. I say nothing. Because I'm too busy biting through the inside of my cheek.

"Good! Complete silence. Good girl," Avian praises with an enormous oblivious smile.

Good. Girl.

This is my fucking life now.

His big palm pats my head affectionately, and I have to stop myself from nipping at his fingers with snapping rage.

The adorable condescending fucker.

He's so smart. But he's so, so damn blind to how much this training is pissing me off.

He sits on the edge of the bed with his legs spread wide as he prepares to click at me once more. If he tells me to sit one more time, I'm going to shove that clicker up his puppy ass.

His thumb lifts, and instead of waiting for the clicking instructions, I stride to him. He can't see me of course, but he instantly notices the sound of my feet storming over the smooth hardwood floors. And he definitely notices when I slide my legs over his, wrap my arms around his shoulders, and just completely straddle him to get his immediate attention.

"Uh—" He's careful. His hands are lifted around me, making it a point not to touch any part of my body that's pressed so perfectly against him. "What are you doing, Cersia?" The groan against his words is just as calm and hushed as he always is. But there's a rawness to it that scratches sensually down over my skin and back.

"Touch my face," I instruct him, and I'm very aware of how hard my lips are down turned and how deep the crease is in my brow.

There's a slowness as he blinks and seems to consider my statement.

I'm his Prince's. That's the label I've acquired, and I know it. Maybe that's why he's kept a careful amount of space between us.

"You don't even know what I look like," I whisper, and that breath of a voice crawls up right from the ache in my soul.

My attention is drawn to his full lips. His hard jaw and the beautiful kindness that's always etched across his face.

He's beautiful.

He's been nothing but caring to me. And for the first time in my life, it isn't because of my looks.

He nods at that. "I know you're the most beautiful woman in all the realms."

"You don't know that."

"I do. I know the rumors of your appearance are true. I know because of how Zilo cautions you like he actually cares if you live or die. And I know because Roman can't stand to be around you for longer than an hour as if that's too much for his self-control to take. They aren't used to being attracted to the Prince's property."

And there it is: I'm property.

I knew I was, but it's still a scraping pain within my chest to hear it spoken aloud.

"Avian." My tongue slides over my lips, and I lean in so close I can taste the apprehension against his lips. "Touch me," I say on more of a gasp than a whisper.

Those words pound over and over within my head the moment I say them.

Touch me. Touch me. Touch me.

And then a rigid hardness is suddenly pressing against me just between my thighs.

There's a gruffness to him as he clears his throat, but he never does avert his silver eyes from mine. Even as his heartbeat lifts to this slamming, demanding pound that matches mine beat for beat.

"Please," I beg in that same desperate tone.

His fingers slide through my blonde locks fast and

hard, gripping the roots in a painful pull. At that, I do gasp. The simple sound of my lust seems to rock through him, and he releases me just as fast as he came. With urgent care, he slides me off his lap and deposits me on the bed before leaping to his feet, adjusting the very thick outline beneath his pants. Then he's fumbling with the door, using that same hand he just owned my body with, and then with what must be a mumbled apology, he's gone.

And I'm left breathlessly staring at that inky door once more.

Alone.

Confused.

And still completely pissed off.

It takes less than an hour for someone to come storming back to me. Where Avian offers me sweet kindness, Zilo is all growling authority, and he's hard to look at.

"Did you fucking come on Avian?" He's screaming at me the moment the door offers us the appearance of privacy.

"Come? What? No!"

"I meant come on to him. Did you come on to him!?"

Wait... "*No*," I affirm all over again.

But...did I?

"No," I say once more. "I wanted him to understand how infuriating this *training* is."

Yes. That was it. Definitely. Originally that was it...I think.

Roman stands at the door, his shoulder leaning into the frame as he crosses one leg over the other in a cockier than ever stance that demands attention. "Next time, try using your mouth. I hear mouths usually talk more than pussy does." His gem-like gaze is a mixture of dead attention and...anger.

He's angry. That aggression lingers there for several seconds before Avian sinks his fist fast and hard into Roman's stomach. The man doubles over instantly without a single groan slipping from his lips.

"Watch your mouth, Roman," Avian warns, and this is the second time I've watched him correct his friend this way.

And I'm still surprised.

They have the strangest affectionately harsh friendship and overwhelming anger I've ever seen.

"It doesn't matter. Don't let it happen again," Zilo warns, his finger pointing at me like he's shaming a puppy instead of a full-grown woman right now.

"Fine." I force a smile to my lips and hold Zilo's hard gaze.

I note the way his attention shifts over my body, my tattered shirt and tight pants. It's a heated, lingering look that he corrects in the blink of any eye.

"She's going to get us all killed," Roman growls.

"No, she won't." Avian shakes his head adamantly,

setting loose some of his shining dark locks into those silver eyes.

A silence falls over the room as the three of them seem to have a passing of words without using actual words. Two of the three still have a heavy furiousness weighting their brows.

As for me, I just wait. I stand trial before these three men who brought me here to help save their kingdom.

Now, they're ready to throw me to the wolves already.

"Get going," Zilo commands without so much as a second glance my way. "Dinner starts in ten minutes."

He's striding out the door and down the darkness of the hall before my mind even processes what that means.

They still want me.

They *need* me anyway.

And that's good enough for now.

SEVEN
BROTHERS

They don't have me change for the royal dinner. The three men dine in nothing but their pants and boots covering their hard bodies. All I can think about is how one hot spill of tea will scar a nipple or two if they're not careful.

Not that I mention it. They're not my nipples to care about after all.

I suppose I just expected more glamour from the kingdom of hell. Instead, I'm surrounded by tattered shirts and blood splattered jeans everywhere I look.

And as for the notorious dark prince, he's nowhere to be seen.

Literally I'm just luncheoning with a few hell fae whose glittering black horns reach high above the crowds, drawing my attention to their depthless onyx eyes and pointed ashen-stained ears. Rows of sharp cutting teeth rip apart their food, and they cackle with laughter and half masticated meat still hanging from their lips as they chatter restlessly with one another.

They're not like the fae my grandmother read to me about. They're not alluring and enchanting at all.

They're fucking terrifying.

"Don't stare," Rome says on a growl of a whisper. He says it while lifting a black cup of ale to his lips and taking a big drink. He drinks for so long my attention lingers on the sharp lines of his jaw...his throat...his—

"I said don't stare," he growls again as he lowers the cup and digs into the meat on his plate.

I avert my eyes to my own plate of charred food. I have no idea what the meat is, and it makes me slightly uncomfortable to know that none of these people care if this is a beef steak or a human steak.

Both options seem feasible.

My shoulders remain squared, my spine hard as I sit like a small child between Zilo's enormous body and Roman's. Their elbows knock into my arms with every bite they take.

Everyone here is animalistic. Including the few half shifters whose tails sweep back and forth behind their chairs. A beautiful woman with big brown eyes and furry fox-like pointed ears sits diagonal from me, just next to Avian, but neither of them speak to one another.

She howls with laughter as the two women across from her snap off line after line about how they ran out to honor the full moon in their human form. Without a stitch of clothing.

I search discreetly from table to table, but I don't spot the white-faced woman with the alarming black lips I met the second I stepped foot here.

I don't know why I look for her, but I do.

The thousands of people in this room, they're happy, but they don't intermingle.

The men around me are High Hell. They should only associate with other High Hell, it seems.

And yet, they're so fucking silent the only words they pass to one another are grunts of approval about the meat they're eating so quickly I swear they're more dog than man at this moment.

Disgusting.

"Good hellish evening, friends," a voice booms over us, raining down on me so hard I feel those words vibrate through my chest in a sense of anxious adrenaline.

There's a quiet that cuts through the darkly lit dining hall. All that manic laughter and scuttling talk ceases to exist, and every eye in the room is lifted to a spot high on the wall that I wasn't even aware of.

Until now. There, cut into the hard stone of the wall, is a jutting balcony. And there, seated on the ground, with his legs hanging carelessly over the edge, is a crowned man who peers down on us.

The Prince of Hell.

"The Honor of the Moon festivities were salacious. A delicious night indeed," the Prince says with a cutting smile slicing his lips. "Soon we will celebrate our new queen, whoever she may be." The heavy attention of the royal man falls hard on me, and I force myself to hold the rigid posture of my confidence in place. "The High Hell have brought me a gift from the moon festivities, it seems," he muses.

The tightness in my chest can only be explained as my body's way of trying to stop my slamming heart from exiting my existence entirely. A chill washes over my skin in a cold douse of clammy anxiety.

Nonetheless, I lift my chin higher and look up at the eerie Prince without an ounce of that fear crawling over the face blessed by the Goddess herself. This is why I'm here: I'm here to seduce the Prince of Hell.

And hope he dies because of my good efforts.

With a leap that disrupts the current of the air in the room, that man pounces down before me. I bite my tongue hard to stop the gasp from leaving my lips as the plates and glasses rattle around him directly in front of me. He balances on the toes of his dirty boots as he hunches down, arms slung over his knees, and he stares wide-eyed at me.

Amazed. He looks at me like someone's bottled dragon's fire and sunk it to the bottom of the sea of Death.

He looks at me the way everyone does.

And I hate it.

"You look enchanting," he whispers, skimming my features with a dark hungry gaze.

A bold idea flickers through my mind, and my hand drifts out between us before I can think better of it. My index finger brushes along his lower lip faintly, but I still feel the heat of his breath rush over my knuckles.

The space between us separates as I lean in to this daunting devilish man and whisper to him and him alone. *"I taste even better."*

A chair scrapes so hard against the floor that the thing falls backward at my side. My attention isn't on the chair though. I watch Roman storm away with lines cut along his back from both scars and tense muscle.

"Roman." The Prince growls out his name with a dusting of sparkling black magic exhaling from his lungs.

And the beautiful, strong man who's warred with me since the moment I met him in the window pane of another realm entirely, he halts.

Freezes actually. Every stiff muscle in his hard body ceases.

And the Prince jumps down and is striding toward him in an instant.

His long fingers taunt over Roman's shoulders as he rounds him and then faces him head-on. "You like the pale woman? Blondes are your type? Sexy blue-eyed vixens are the key to your weak little soul?" The cutting smile on his lips makes me sick.

Or maybe the twisting of my stomach is because of the belittling way he's talking to Roman...

"You think you're deserving of such a luxury as a woman?" The Prince is so focused on Roman that his inky black eyes shine with excitement and danger.

I hate him.

I hate this man, and I know nothing about him.

"Come here." He points at the spot just near his side. Everyone in the room passes a look.

To me.

He's talking to me.

Even if he never so much as glances my way.

I'm standing without a second's hesitation, and despite the seriousness slicing into this moment, I just know Avian is beaming with pride all because I followed a simple order.

Stop smiling, asshole.

It wasn't some great accomplishment.

I do listen...ish.

The impassive look on my face is held tightly in place with a carelessness I'm summoning deep from my hard pounding heart.

It feels like every step is leaden. Time passes like I'm looking back on a decade of tragedy instead of ten seconds of casual walking.

And then I'm locking eyes with the cruelest gaze filled with so much manic destruction.

"Tell me, my sweet, is Roman appealing?" the Prince of Hell asks.

The use of that nickname slides over me like cold vomit hitting my face.

I smile the most charmed smile.

"Women do not love the weak," I answer without hesitancy, and it hurts. It hurts so fucking much to say what I know he wants to hear.

Yesterday I held this man in my arms, and today I tell him he's worthless.

If I wasn't already in hell, I'd have just reserved my seat with that single comment alone.

It works perfectly though. The corner of the Prince's mouth angles up in a hard, pleased smirk.

"Beauty and brains. No wonder my brother likes you."

Brother.

That word circles over and over and over again, and I grow sicker and sicker with each and every round it makes. Roman is the Prince of Hell's own flesh and blood.

And judging by last night's whippings, I'd say he's punished frequently simply because of that blood.

I don't dare look at him. As tight as my throat is and as painful as my heart feels, I won't dare risk a look at him.

"Kiss him," the Prince says suddenly, his words ringing out among the watchful crowd, and I nearly stumble in my desire to look to Zilo for guidance.

I don't. I hold that charmed dazed smile in place and try to blaze through all the possible outcomes of this test.

Is it a test? For me? Or for Roman?

I should refuse. I should appear appalled.

But to be uncertain is to fail.

And I don't fail.

I turn on my heels, and my lips lock with the softest

waiting mouth. I expect no reaction from the magically bound man held in place.

To my surprise, his warm tongue slides over my lips. And I open to him in a gasp of surprise and need. Strong fingers shove through my long hair, and he pulls me to him harder, kissing me so deeply he steals the air in my lungs.

Along with every logical thought that was previously occupying my dense little brain.

A growling groan turns to agony so fierce I can taste it against his tongue. Every part of his body tenses as some kind of pain takes over. But still he kisses me like I'm the only thing keeping him from dying.

It's the strangest thing to feel like someone needs you. It isn't like being wanted at all.

Desire. Longing. Lust.

They're nothing compared to love.

And that's oddly what this demanding passionate kiss feels like.

And that's why I jerk away from him, shoving my hands between us to accommodate even more space between me and that consuming sensation of being cherished. The moment I do, he falls to his knees. His head lowers, and he trembles in torment, curling up on his side as unseen violence rains down on him.

"She tasted good, did she? The things you can't have always taste the best." The Prince's smile is still in place, and his eyes burn with shining magic as he glares down on the man lying at his feet.

"Fucking delicious," Roman taunts, his own smile curling his lips through the pain that covers his face. "I bet when you finally taste her, she'll taste like mine," he spits just before a hard tremble overtakes him and he swallows back a scream stuck in his throat.

It's that comment that finally shatters the amusement in the Prince's eyes. With a deadly scowl, his boot collides with Roman's ribs, and then he turns abruptly away before the gasping pain even leaves his brother's mouth. Prince Ravar storms through the aisle without looking back. "Punishment, Zilo! Punishment!" he beckons over his shoulder before shoving open the heavy double doors and exiting entirely.

I stand there looking at one man while worrying over another. I don't help Rome. I can't.

Instead, I walk right back to my seat with that sickness clawing at my stomach. With all eyes on me, I cling to that unimpressed look hiding my emotions.

And then I pick up that disgusting fucking meat.

And I eat it.

I eat it like I belong here.

I eat it like I love it here.

I eat it like I'm the most devout little follower of the Prince of Hell.

And later, when I'm finally alone, I'll vomit all of the disturbing things I've taken in tonight right back up.

EIGHT

IT'S GETTING HARD

It's odd to be alone in the night. The three of them never came to bed. And I never slept.

So I wait. My legs are curled tightly beneath the gown that I came here in. It's thin and tattered, but it gives me a weird little sense of comfort that I didn't know I needed until now. It doesn't relax me enough to ease how hard my hands are clinging to my arms as I hold myself on the small black velvet settee. The pretty cloth no longer smells like mother. The scent of cold ash stains its threads.

It stains me.

What in the fucking Goddess Moon's name am I doing here? An adventure? I thought this shit was going to be an adventure? A fucking purpose?

I was wrong.

I was so damn wrong it's insulting how easily I

walked away from a good family. A kind man. And a safe pack who never truly knew me.

The sound of hinges whining doesn't catch my attention. The heavy fall of footsteps clumping over dark hardwood floors doesn't so much as scratch at the back of my messy thoughts. His warm hand gently pressing to my collarbone, along the fine flesh there, that's what draws me to the serious eyes that hold...*concern?*

Could Zilo dare to be concerned when he has so much asshole-iness to attend to?

"Why are you awake?" That gravelly tone of his is warm instead of gruff. It's a delicious melody that washes over my body and floods out the anxiety in my mind.

Almost...

"Did you do it?" My gaze narrows up at him as I hold myself harder.

"Do what?"

I swallow stiffly and try to make it simple for this fucker to understand. "Did. You. Punish. Him?" My eyebrow arches so high it's painful.

I wait patiently, but passive-aggressively, for his reply.

He doesn't even blink. "Yes."

Of course he fucking did!

I'm on my feet and right in his personal space, storming even closer so fast he barely backsteps every step I take. Until there are no more. And he's pinned right up against the wall. And I don't hesitate to keep going. On the tips of my toes and with my chin held high,

I meet his gaze with just a breadth of space separating my lips from his.

"How can you call yourself a pack and harm him day in and day out? How the fuck can you live with yourself? How has no one plotted your death along with the Prince's?" My jaw hurts from how tightly I snap it closed, and somewhere between us, my index finger found a bit of hard muscle, and I suppose I've been poking his stone wall chest with every word I've said.

I honestly have no idea other than the fact that my finger kind of hurts now.

And that alone should tell me to back down from this deadly hellhound of a man.

It's just too bad that that logic hasn't caught up with my rage yet.

"Cersia," he whispers calmly, "do not finger fuck my chest *again*." His jaw, like my own, twitches with a hidden hinting aggression. It's a warning sign like wolves' hair lifting from the back of their neck just before they strike.

Fuck his aggression.

My arm rears back, and all the shaking emotional anger I've held onto for the past several hours storms forward with the tiniest little poke that holds so much meaning.

And that's all it takes.

All that composure Zilo holds on to when I'm around comes crashing down as his arms grip around me, his chest collides with my body, and he spins me so fast the entire room is a blur of darkness. Until my cheek cracks against the smooth wall, and his chest presses down against my back. My hands are held tightly from behind in one of his big paws. A knee comes up high, and he separates my stance with a quick shove of his thigh between my legs. Steady fingers slide through my hair, and he tilts my head just the way he wants so his gaze is in my peripheral.

"You're entirely too reckless for someone who can't even manage her own beast within herself. Are you going to calm your little ass down now?" His voice is so mellow and at ease it just pisses me off how much harder I'm breathing.

"Fuck you and your obsession with my ass." I literally spit at him. Of course, my retaliation spittle just falls against my own shoulder, but it feels good to do it anyway.

His grip against my hair as well as my wrists tightens, and he pulls my head back against him while crushing my hips into the wall. My mouth falls open from how hard he's angling my throat. The rough brush of his beard skims along my jawline.

"If your attitude threatens our plans, I won't ask the others for advice. I'll kill you to save ourselves. I won't hesitate."

I barely move against his hold, but ever so slightly I twist my wrists, adjusting just subtly and just enough to rock the curve of my ass against the most sensitive part of this insensitive man.

And then I'm speechless for another reason.

The hardness that grinds up against me as he pushes me down once more must be a surprise for him as much as it is for me.

Because he shuts right the fuck up.

And yet, he's too arrogant to release me.

So he clears his throat harshly, but he keeps his hard length snuggled nicely against my ass. And I bite back the laugh lodged in my throat at how much he can curse and stomp around and fight anyone who might threaten his poor fragile ego.

But one nice ass is all it takes for him to lose his composure.

I mean, it is an ass blessed by the Goddess, but come on, man.

My spine arches from how hard I lift up and then ever so slowly lower back down.

"Stop," he grinds out.

And I too grind.

All. Over. Again.

With force, he pulls my hair and yanks me harder. I gasp, and I think that just makes it—yeah, it makes it harder for him...

"I said stop it!"

"Then stop fucking tormenting your friends!" I growl right back at him.

"That's not what we're talking about, and you know it!" he whisper-screams in my ear, all hot and bothered and so, so sexy.

"Really? Then what are we talking about, Zilo? Tell me." My fingers spread wide, and I'm shocked at how slow he is to pull away as my nails drag over the hard outline in his pants. But he does pull away. He puts so much space between us I bet he'd solicit the Goddess herself to take pity on his hellish soul and pull him away from this realm entirely if he could.

A tic in his jaw pulses with rage or lust, or maybe that's his disturbing orgasm face for all I know. But he's definitely fuming at me, for good or bad reasons is anyone's guess.

"I-I," he stutters, not even able to get two words out before he's pacing the room on booming steps. "I'll deter Prince Ravar's commands for punishment as much as I can."

"And I'll deter my *attitude* as much as I can," I say with poised rationality.

A pressing memory of how good he felt against me lingers in my mind.

Those heavy, prying eyes of his skim my features, searching me out while I simply gaze back at his barbaric disbelief.

"Fine." He nods once.

I nod.

He does it again.

I do it once more.

And by his third time of him rattling his little puppy dog brain, it occurs to me that he's still thinking about it.

And now I am too.

I'm seducing the Prince of Hell.

It's my job.

At the moment though, I'm mentally undressing the Highest High Hell of the Prince's guard. Even worse, he's eye fucking me right back.

It's a flame of heat to feel his attention warm against my skin. The memory of his body pressing down on mine feels like the weight is still there. The spot where his knee parted my thighs is fresh in my mind, and that pressure too is still present against my core.

Too, too present.

"You should leave," I blurt suddenly.

His eyes widen as if I just threatened him.

"It's my fuckin' room," he argues.

Why is he like this? Why?

"Do you want us to fuck and die of treason, or would you rather we continue our fun plot to kill the Prince?" My hands lift at my sides as if I hold the two offers there in my palms, and it's like he actually sees them now that I've mentioned it.

"Yeah, I should go," he says, striding to the glossy black door before the words are fully out of his mouth.

The door slams behind without him so much as tossing a second glance my way. It doesn't hurt to watch him go.

It hurts to watch myself continue to shove away all of the good men in my life.

And for what?

A sense of purpose.

It's what my father would be proud of. Bringing down the leader of this realm is indeed what my father would have wanted for my future.

I just have to keep reminding myself of that every single time one of these men gets close to me.

It's an impossible future I've set out for.

Killing the Prince is only the half of it.

NINE
WAKE-UP CALL

I sleep alone. It's peaceful, and I'm used to it. I enjoy it. Especially in a bed the size of a small country.

It's wonderful to fall asleep that way really.

Until my eyes open slowly to find a man gazing down on me with unseeing eyes.

"Why's Zilo acting nice?" Avian asks with total suspicion clouding his silver orbs.

My lips twitch, but the smile doesn't fully form.

Nice. Hmmm. Who would have thought niceness actually existed in that man?

"I have no idea." The words tumble out on a yawn accompanied by a long and possibly stalling stretch that gives me the chance to avoid those sightless, prying eyes.

I feel him studying me. He's picking apart my silence, my body movement, my fucking breathing, heartbeat and probably the fall of my lashes with every blink I take.

But I'm innocent.

I give him nothing.

When I'm done dragging out my morning leg, ankle, and toe stretches, I lazily look back at him. Narrowed attention is still held intently on me.

His hair's shaved along the sides, and the thick single braid that pulls back against his head is perfectly put together. He's flawlessly shaved the dark stubble along his square jaw. Not a hair is out of place.

And I know he's as aware of everyone around him as much as he is of himself.

I just don't understand his intuition whatsoever.

It's shocking to say the least.

"You came on to him and tricked him into this forced weird niceness," he speculates.

And holy fuck.

Fucking shocking.

How does he know that?

Why does it sound creepy when he says it like that?

"I did not!" As soon as I speak, I wish I could take back the outrage in my voice and spew it back out into a sound of honest composure instead of a yapping dog whose tail just got stepped on.

"Oh, you did." He nods like it's all clear and coming together now.

He leans in closer on the messy bedspread to really analyze—whatever the fuck it is that gives him the sixth, seventh, and eighth senses.

Is he a guilt whisperer? A shame senser? A sex seeker?

Side note: if he's looking for that last one, I'm offering.

Focus, Cersia!

I blink the mystery of his knowledge away and lean up in bed to really talk to him like an adult and not a pouting child caught in her lies.

"I told Zilo to stop the punishments." I lift my chin high without remorse.

I did a good fucking deed.

And I wake to be interrogated for it.

"That was a bad idea, Cers." He shakes his head back and forth, and I hate how much these ridiculous men fight to hold on to the pain in their lives.

But I do get it.

"I'm not telling him to disobey the Prince. I asked him to just...avoid the punishments. I-I hate seeing what it does to Roman, and even if he won't show it, I know it hurts Zilo. He's not as unbreakable as he acts."

A beat of silence thrums between us, and when I look back at him, his gaze isn't searching. It's tragic.

"She told us you were beautiful. She didn't say you were kind," he whispers.

My heart skips and stutters as it tries to find its pace while I fall into the deep depths of his gaze.

"The witch?" I ask starstruck.

He nods.

"I want to meet her." I should have met her from the start. She's the reason I'm here. She should have met me at the fucking door.

"You already did. At the entryway."

That was the witch?

Oh. Okay. I guess she did meet me at the door. Maybe I'll calm down a minute.

"She was the eerie face in the darkness..." I try to think it all through, but she just saw me and barely lingered before she left again.

As if ninth-sensing my confusion, Avian says, "She isn't welcomed in this kingdom. The Prince, he—he would kill her if he saw her."

"I suppose she might really bring down the mood of this enthusiastic place with her talk of a peaceful future." I blink away my annoyance at missing my chance to question the Night Witch.

"You'll see her again," Avian answers on that I'm-In-Your-Head voice he always seems to have.

"Good," I say with a tired sigh.

"Now get up. If I have to put up with Zilo's creepy niceness, then so do you." He waves his hand in a circular *let's get on with it* sort of way.

My head hits the pillow, and I barely close my eyes for the briefest moment before a big hand is wrapped around my ankle. And then I'm being pulled.

"Dammit, Avian!" I'm jerked through the cold unused sheets all the way to the very edge of the bed where he pauses.

And then jerks once more.

My ass hits the hard floors without so much as a bounce.

I blink up at the man who I thought so highly of since the moment we met. "I thought you were the nice one," I grumble, my words fanning the long blonde hair that's tangled in front of my face.

A warm and delicious sound of amusement touches his lips, and I couldn't be mad at him if I wanted to. And damn do I want to.

He lowers swiftly, balancing on the toes of his boots, and I can't help the way my attention veers right down to the hard panes of his stomach that are now at eye level with me. He gets good and close.

His fingers lightly push my hair from my face, and I swear he has a third eye.

Shit, now that sounds dirty too.

I hold his pretty, steely eyes, and it's intimate the way he gazes at me with hardly any space lingering between us. His head dips low, and his smooth jaw skims mine as his mouth grazes the shell of my ear.

"Didn't anyone warn you? None of us are nice, Cers," he whispers like dark sex and blinding orgasms.

Then he's on his feet in a matter of seconds. And my mouth's still open as I stare after him.

Fuck.

TEN

THAT PANTY INTUITION

THE VOICES I hear when I step into what Avian calls the Formal Torture Room, are more mellow than I had expected from a place called the *Formal Torture Room*. Screaming? I suppose I expected a little screaming. Maybe some crying. A bit of begging added for dramatic flair.

But no, they really missed the mark when they originally titled this space.

"I'm not telling you what to do, Rome. I'm just suggesting, maybe from here on out, you don't kiss the Prince's property," Zilo explains in a therapeutic way.

When I enter from the hall, the two of them are seated in black chairs that appear to have dried blood staining them. An array of fancy cutting knives lies between them on a metallic tray. They're unused, shining and clean. Ropes, chains, barbed wire and a weird collection of broom handles line the smooth walls.

"I appreciate that suggestion, my friend," Roman taunts with a wide smile stretched across his perfect white teeth so hard that he looks manic, "but have you thought about maybe not grinding your cock against the Prince's property as well?"

A big fist slams down on the table between them, rattling the tempting knives briefly before Zilo catches his temper. He pushes back his long black hair, and that's when I notice he's wearing thin black frames.

Glasses. He's actually wearing glasses. And talking like a therapist...

What fucking realm of hell have I fallen into this morning?

"I did not grind my cock into her—it was—it was a misunderstanding," he says on a calming but shaking exhale.

Avian arches a brow at me, but I ignore the little knowing bastard's look and continue to watch quietly from the door.

"So I won't kiss her, and you won't...accidently misunderstand where your cock belongs?" Roman tilts his head to the side and waits smugly for his friend's response.

Goddess, they're insufferable to one another.

"Exactly." Zilo nods over and over again. So much so that it's a hypnotic repetition like he's trying to cast a spell to make the words real.

I can practically picture the carousel of chanting now:

I won't use my cock for good deeds. I won't use my cock for good deeds. I won't use my cock for good deeds.

I can't take it anymore.

They're exhausting.

"All settled then?" I ask in the most announcing voice I possess.

Zilo jolts in his chair while Roman simply passes his gaze my way. They both stare hard at me for so long that it's difficult not to shift beneath their warm attention.

"I thought you were entertaining the Prince this morning," Zilo asks with more anger than I've heard in his tone since I walked into this so called Formal Torture Room.

"No..." I hang on the confusion of his question, and it only seems to crease his smooth bronze skin with a look of panic.

"Fuck."

Fuck indeed.

I stand surrounded by the three concerned looking men in the dark hall.

They're concerned partly because I'm here, and partly because someone a bit more vocal is in there.

Her moans are a drowning thing. More performance than pleasure. Higher and higher, her screams echo. Unsteadily they fall until she seems to remember her role she's playing, and then they pitch all over again.

"Oh, just come already. It's sex not a theater production," I complain.

Zilo nudges me to quiet down as the four of us lurk outside the Prince's chambers. "Shh," he hisses.

I roll my eyes.

"As if anyone could hear us right now. The wolves in my realm are probably picking up on Moaning Martha in there." My arms fold hard.

"Are you jealous?" Romey asks, leaning against the wall at my side as he folds his arms and really studies me.

"Uh, I guess I'm supposed to be. Yeah. So jealous right now."

His smirk that's normally so cruel is almost infectious. It pulls at my own lips simply from seeing him smile. He so rarely really smiles. He smirks and cackles all day but so seldomly ever seems happy.

"You should be jealous," Zilo snaps, ripping the meager happiness right from us. "You're losing, Cersia."

Losing. Wow. Okay. I hadn't realized a one-night stand was the prize here.

"She should be about in the mornings," Avian advises.

What does that even mean? *Be about what in the mornings.* Be about what?

"Yeah, and she should wear more perfume. It's about the pheromones," Roman adds with a glint in his pale green eyes that tells me he's being a total cock eater right now.

"That's a good idea," Zilo says while pushing his

glasses up to really think this puzzle out. "Maybe tighter pants. Tight pants are always good on a mate. Shows the bearing hips."

Bearing hips?

The three of them nod dickishly in unison.

"No underwear too," Roman adds to my list with another exaggerated I'm-A-Fucking-Tool nod.

"How do you know the difference?" Avian asks.

"It's a panty intuition. You wouldn't get it," Roman says without hesitation and total honesty.

Panty. Intuition.

Give me a fucking break.

I glare at his obnoxiously pretty face. Him and his besties are a happy little triad of stupidity. And I'm just the voyeuristic idiot watching as they thoroughly fuck me into another bad idea.

"Maybe I should forgo the clothes entirely," I suggest with a shrug.

"That might help, really." Roman's eat-shit smile is so taunting it's infuriatingly cute.

It's a nice reminder that I still hate him.

Intensely.

"Ya know, I'll figure out how to get the petty attention of a Prince myself. I don't need your puppy clicker training on how to make a man notice me. Thanks." I'm walking away while they're mumbling between dramatic sex noises about how women are oblivious to what men *really* want.

Like it's hard.

ELEVEN
DUELING SEDUCTION

Zilo explains to me that the Prince of Hell has a very elaborate morning schedule:

Fucking.

Eating.

Dueling.

Yes, men are complex creatures indeed.

And that's why I'm lingering in the shadows of the dueling arena for his guard to take the final blow and bow out of the current match Prince Ravar is kicking his ass in. Finally—fucking finally—the guard takes a hard fall to the black soot, puffs of glittering dirt fanning up around him.

And he doesn't get up as the Prince pins his shining onyx blade to the center of the stocky man's burly throat.

"Good move, my Prince," the guard comments respectfully.

The Prince's smile is a cutting thing. Almost as sharp

as his weapon. It should signal what comes next. But it doesn't.

The blade hauls back, and with as much force as he can muster, Prince Ravar rails the metal clean through the man's chest.

An empty breath is the only sound as the dozens of spectators watch their leader murder his own guard right before their eyes. The man's gaze is big and terrified as he clings to the blade impaling him, and he stares up at the one person who should have his best interest at heart.

And I wonder if that's what he's thinking just as the shining light in his eyes fades out.

My own heart tightens, and the air in my lungs has been missing for a long moment now.

It hurts.

But I can't pause.

I can't stop the charade for even a second.

Because like Roman said, I'm losing. And that means I'm failing men just like this guard.

With my head held high, I stride out into the ashen arena. I feel the attention of the royals and the kingdom above watching every step I take out toward the cruel man wiping fresh blood from his blade.

"He wasn't really much of an opponent," I say with the nastiness of those words stinging my tongue.

The Prince turns, and I know the moment he really sees me. Because that sheer mating gown is finally coming in handy. He seems to note the way it clings to the flawless shape of my breasts and the nice curve of my hips.

While the men wanted me to blend in to this culture of practicality in their dark pants and worn shirts, that's not what will get me noticed.

And I am being thoroughly fucking noticed right now.

"Good morning," he says with a heat in his eyes I've seen too many times to count.

I've also seen the way men's eyebrows shoot up high when I pick up a weapon. Just like his does as I pick up the dead man's blade. I study the length of it. Not a drop of blood adorns the dark metal. Not one wound was given to the guard's killer.

We should rectify that.

I hold the hilt in my palm in a sort of novice way. I'll admit I like to play innocent from time to time... Okay, so I like to fuck with people sometimes. Nothing wrong with that.

I peer up from beneath my thick lashes at the man watching me with insulting amusement in his features. "You're a cute one," he labels me. *Cute*. I'ma be so damn cute when I cut your dick from your balls.

"Thank you, my Prince." The smile I give him is that same innocence. "Care to go another round?" With purpose, I flop my sword around in a mock of a joust.

Ah, he laughs and laughs. Like a total fucking fool.

"I'd love to go a few rounds with you," he insinuates with a rake of his gaze sliding down my frame once more.

To really stroke his ego, I appraise him right back. I measure up all the ways he's different from Roman. They're brothers, but the similarity in appearance is very vague. The inky black hair that's pushed back from his face is the only matching trait I can pinpoint. And even that's hard since Roman is shaved closely. The gaze eating me up right now isn't alight with energy. It's dark and haunting. Even his build is opposing to Roman's tall lithe frame. The Prince stands just a few small inches taller than myself.

And that will make him an excellent opponent to duel this morning.

"Ready?" I ask with another haphazardly floppy cock wave of my weapon.

He smiles that amused little smirk once more at my attempt to play with men's toys. "I won't kill you, Cersia. I'll be gentle with you."

Goddess, he's obnoxious.

This will be fun.

I smirk at him as I pull one leg back and position my weight to balance out the strike I'm already intending. The simple change in my stance puts a confused crease between his thick eyebrows.

It's the most rewarding fucking look of concern.

My arm flexes as I truly take hold of the hilt of the sword and lower it until I'm ready. Until he's ready. Fuck, he better be ready.

A rumbling murmur carries around the shadowed

THE DARKEST WOLVES

arena, but one voice calls out above all others. "Is everything alright here, my Prince?"

Zilo's question doesn't distract me, but I do take a quick moment to toss him a *get the fuck out* glare from over my shoulder.

Zilo's serious attention slides from me to Ravar and then back again.

A slight *what in the High Hell fuck are you doing* sort of look arches in his brow.

If it helps, I'm not wearing panties like they told me to. Damn. Be appreciative. I followed your advice. And no one seems to care.

"It is more than alright, Zilo. I was just about to show Lady Cersia a move or two." The way he licks his lips after that causes my gag reflex to wave at me from the back of my throat.

"Fuck," I hear a familiar voice whispers like a threat.

I just hope Roman notices I took the panty advice. Hello. I'm fucking trying here.

"She wore the perfume," Avian says sweetly.

Thank you!

Thank you, Avian! Goddess, would it kill the other two to notice the effort from time to time?

Anyway.

I toss my long blonde hair over my shoulder and roll my neck back and forth in a coy little way that draws the Prince's attention back to me. Finally. Let's get back to business.

The delicate, discreet muscles of my shoulder blades

tense, my wrist poises, my entire body ever so subtly falls into place, mirroring all the training my father taught me so, so long ago. Some things you never forget. Seven years have passed since he cheered me on to take the fight with my blade rather than my teeth.

Never rely on your hidden beast to shift.

You can only count on yourself and your ability.

And my ability, it's fucking flawless.

I never make a move. I don't dare reveal my hand until he's lunging forward with a light-hearted downward arch of his blade. It slams against mine in the softest touch of metal meeting metal.

But he clearly expected the meager weight of his attack to rattle my hold on my weapon. At least, that's what the highbrowing shock on his face is telling me.

I smile.

He hesitates.

It's the most delicious moment of being unsuspecting, innocent, and so, so *beautiful*.

And then I attack.

Both hands clamp the hilt, and I fling his weight off of the shine of my blade. He staggers back, but I keep on going. I don't pause for a single second as I eat up the space between him and me, and he barely has a single second to react before I swing the cutting edge right back at him.

It misses his bare, sweaty chest with a whisper of air. And that confusion in his eyes turns to erotic fury. The Prince dances with me in a give and take of near fatal dips and dives of our weapons. The danger and the adrenaline of it all exhilarates me as much as it seems to enthrall him.

It's the strangest happiness two people have ever found in trying to murder one another.

And then, my sword flings forward once more, and the very tip of the weapon scratches over his shoulder.

A gasp of fear and surprise sounds through our audience who I had briefly forgotten. The way no one says a word but echoes their panic in that single gasp drills anxiety all through my chest. I've never been apprehensive of harming an opponent before.

But I've made a mistake.

In the thrill of the fight, I forgot my place. And I definitely forgot about the man lying dead just yards away, simply because he lost too humbly.

"Cersia," Roman whispers on a chill of a word that I feel spoken fearfully across my skin even with the span of space separating us.

I am going to die now.

The Prince's black orbs lift from his slight wound to meet my wide eyes. His chest rises and falls with the effort of our battle still relevant on his face.

I can't even think in this moment.

The heavy weight of his steps billows clouds of dark smoke around his footfalls, and I'm entranced by the hellish appearance he's creating all around him. I can't see anything but this evil man.

He is the last face I'll ever see before I die.

With one swift move, he brings his arm back, lifting his blade with intent.

Then he tosses it to the side, grabs my neck and drags me against him.

Just as his lips crash down on mine. His kiss consumes the confusion lingering on my tongue, in my chest, in the dark depths of the back of my mind.

It isn't sweet. It isn't sexy.

Where his brother kissed me with so much passion, Ravar kisses me with possession. He kisses me like I'm a prop for him to use and abuse, and I know it in the simple way he devours my mouth for his own pleasure. Even as I choke on his tongue.

And he keeps right on going.

My brain catches up, and I force myself to react. I force my hands to push through his hair. I pull just hard enough to hear his groan against my mouth.

I react how I know he expects me to.

How everyone expects me to.

But he tastes like rancid ash. He tastes like a tormentor. Like an abuser. Like a killer.

That's why I kiss him back too.

Because, in the end, that's exactly why I'm here—to attract a killer.

So far, so good.

TWELVE
THE PLOT THICKENS

"You're brilliant," Zilo says with the biggest smile I've ever seen the brooding man possess.

He's...cute when he smiles.

The approval on his face sears through my chest like warm chocolate, and I can't explain why he has that effect on me suddenly.

Strange indeed.

"Thank you," I beam at him, and Avian nods along with his normal sweet, sincere smile.

Too bad when I peer over at the third little puppy, he isn't as kind.

"Could have gotten yourself killed," Roman spits, his arms folding hard over his bare chest as he looks me up and down.

"And you three could have made me look better instead of trying to cock block my bonding time."

"Bonding time!" Rome lashes out and is storming

over to me from across the bedroom with rage booming into his every step.

Each of these men have a love-hate relationship with logic. Logic tumbles out, and rage rolls right on in during the blink of an eye.

It's true for Roman, and it's true even for Avian. Speaking of, Avian flashes between myself and his friend so fast I don't know if I could spot his superhuman speed if he warned me first.

Not that he ever does.

His palms slam into Roman's chest, and his fingers spread wide as the two of them seethe unshed aggression into the heated breaths between them.

"Move," is all Roman says on a gravelly growl.

Avian's glare becomes slightly less violent, and his silver eyes sparkle with the affection he always hoards in that shining knight heart of his.

"Calm down," Avian whispers, and I can feel the moment his hands turn from being a defense stance to an intimate stance. It's in how the tension in his hard lined shoulders and back melt into total calm. It's like he just wants to feel Roman's heartbeat against his fingertips rather than nearly shoving him away.

Maybe it's both.

Roman's pale eyes are still hard piercing when he looks at me from over his friend's shoulder. I hold that stare for as long as he lets me. I hold it for so long the anger between us fades, edging little by little into begrudging understanding.

But the real thing is, why does he care? Why does he care if I die? If I die, they continue on. They find a new me. And their ultimate goal is still intact.

I'm the one risking something.

I have a purpose here. And I'm not about to fail it.

"We need real plotting. I need in on the actual destination for this little adventure you've pulled me in to."

"No," Zilo says, surprising me with the gruff rumble of his tone that I had nearly forgotten he was capable of. We were making such progress with his kindness.

Where are his glasses? Why has he taken off his reading glasses that were clearly what helped with his personality.

Right now, it's shit. This personality is shit; I much prefer the other.

"No?" I cock my head to the right like I can't fathom holding it up while he disrespects me so blatantly.

"No," he enunciates. "You're not authorized. Another person knowing our full plan, is another person willing to repeat it."

"You think I'd rat on you?"

The synchronization of all three men shrugging at the same time burns disgust all through me.

Wow.

I expected this childish distrust from Roman. Maybe from Zilo too if I'm honest...but Avian? Avian doesn't trust me.

I may as well be alone here.

"You three came to me. I didn't beg you to take me to

the fucking pits of hell."

"Might as well have. What else did you have waiting in your future?" Roman cuts that statement out so hard it hurts. It sinks into my chest like a knife with the honesty of it all bleeding into me.

"Fuck you." My jaw grinds shut, and I want nothing more than to kick him in his dick and walk away.

But I have nowhere to walk to.

And it's clear Roman's entirely dickless anyway.

"We should give our report." Avian doesn't look at me when he says those quiet little words, but I can see the guilt in his gray eyes.

Good.

He should feel guilty.

Zilo though, he's staring at me like he finally wants to call a truce. The set of his lips is uneasy like he wishes to say more but he doesn't possess the kind of words I'd want to hear.

And we both know that.

Finally, Zilo gives in. He does. He just does it wrong. And instead of amending the broken relationship we've never fixed, he turns away and leads the other two men out to give that Goddessdamn important High Hell report.

One by one they exit through the glossy door frame. It's a slow leave of them walking away, so slow that Roman has time to glance back my way, his lips parting without sound. The hurt in the room is a living, breathing thing that presses against my chest.

Does it press against his too?

His attention stays locked on me, his hand lingering on the doorknob.

Say something!

Anything.

Say fucking anything.

Please.

He lazily pulls the handle, and the door glides closed behind them with a quiet whispered click.

Then the dampness in my eyes hits my cheeks, and I can't seem to stop it all from coming. The pressure in my chest is too much and forces out the tears faster and faster until I can't hear anything but my racing pulse in my ears.

"I shouldn't have come here," I scold myself.

"Yes, you should have," an ominous faraway voice answers.

My shoulders tense as my hands fist at my sides, and I'm on the defense in the silent bedroom.

Alone.

The beast deep inside me vibrates against my chest with a roaring warning that doesn't translate against my lips. I suddenly wish my father wasn't so adamant about hiding my natural form. I should have shifted at a young age and embraced that side of me.

But now I'm twenty-one, and the creature is lost inside myself.

And I'm just a fool for thinking my own strength is enough in a realm of immeasurable power.

I scan the room from left to right. The dark colors of

the walls, the floors, the furniture and bedding, it all bleeds into one blanket of blackness. Nothing's there.

Her face flashes white right in front of me, and I lash out without hesitation. The sting of my palm against her face is a snapping sound.

I flinch harder than she does from the realization of what I've done.

I slapped the Night Witch...

Fuck.

Her pencil thin eyebrows lift high, and she blinks away whatever she feels from the hard sting of my skin against hers.

"I-I'm sorry, Creatchin," I say with my shoulders held tight and my words tasting far more formal than I've ever tried to be in my entire life.

"Don't be." A hint of a smile pulls at her black lips. "Don't ever be sorry, Cersia. Don't drown in your emotions of uncertainty. Uncertainty solves nothing! Actions do." Her thin hands fold one over the other, and I notice how slender her frame is and how beautiful the glittering black lace is that covers her in a wafting floor length gown.

In a way, she's beautiful. And tragic. That tragic beauty is a haunting image to stare dead in the face. Is that what I'll become as well as the years pass by: a tragic beauty?

"So." She seats herself at the center of the velvet settee, long legs crossing in a fluid motion that sways her gown. "What's your plan, Cersia?"

I don't reply but simply let that question grow in my mind until it fills every little space of my thoughts.

"*My* plan..." Images of how easily I could gain the Prince's trust spark one after the other behind my eyes. "It isn't my plan." I answer instead.

Because it's not. This isn't my war. It's theirs, and I'm here to help.

I want to help.

"You know as well as I do, you're the heart of this little plot they've created. Tell me what the heart wants." Long black hair cascades around her sharp features as she looks at me like an alluring nightmare.

"I want to be useful. I want purpose—"

"Lies!" She snaps the word out in a rattling tone, but her features remain stony and poised. "Everyone wants something. Even if they don't know it yet."

It feels like an accusation, but what she's accusing doesn't immediately settle in, it slams in. And it occurs to me so suddenly that my brows rise high. "You think I want the crown of hell?"

Thin eyebrows lift on her pale face in a sort of questioning *don't you* appearance.

"I don't want to be queen of this realm that I know very little about." And what I do know, it isn't looking fucking good here.

Goddess no. I don't want this responsibility.

"Then think about who should have the crown." She waits patiently, but it's like she's leading me around to answer the questions she knows all the answers to.

With heavy confusion clouding my thoughts, I actually take a moment to consider what I do know about the realm of hell...

The Prince is a deadly asshole... The people live in tattered clothes and could be better taken care of... The dynamics of the guards—the High Hell—it's a nice set up, but the proud warriors abuse one another all because the Prince is obviously threatened by his brother—*shit. His brother*.

"Roman," I whisper like a treasonous sin.

Her eyes widen with a glinting knowing look.

She brought me here because Roman should own the crown. I can help him do that. But the three of them are constantly watching their backs.

As they should.

One wrong move, and they could all be murdered for their crimes against Prince Ravar.

Unless someone else does their dirty work for them.

It all clatters into place in my messy thoughts.

"I'm going to kill the Prince." I look up at her suddenly, and those thin black painted lips carve up in a pleased smile.

"Good." That smile widens until vicious, inky teeth reveal her happiness. "And I'll help you."

A revelation blooms in my chest, and I too smile quietly back at her.

Good.

Good indeed.

THIRTEEN
THEN THERE WERE THREE

It takes no more than three days for me to go from eating greasy pork/beef/human meat among the others to dining at the Prince's side, sipping from his glass still held intimately in his hand, and finally, being invited to a private evening.

My stomach turns sickly the moment Avian tells me the good news.

"He wants to see you," he repeats as we linger on the sidelines of the arena. Two men fling their weapons in violent blows at one another while I imagine the violent blows the Prince might have in mind for the two of us tonight.

This is what I worked for. This is what I wanted.

I should be happy.

"I think I'm going to be sick." My palm falls to the exposed skin between my pants and tight shirt, and Roman's attention follows that move.

The concern is there in his bright brooding eyes. Zilo seems oblivious or simply caught within the darkness of his own mind. And yet, we all hold our silence.

We let these thoughts fester until they're bleeding out and drowning us in the darkness of what's to come. I hate it. I hate pretending, and I hate feeling nauseated by what all my pretending is leading to.

But I can't stop.

Not until that man is dead and the rightful ruler is crowned.

I don't realize I'm still staring at Roman until he clears his throat harshly and quickly looks away... He was staring at me just like I was staring at him.

Maybe both of us feel that pressing dagger that's stuck through my throat and heart.

I swallow down the pain of it all, and I don't say another word before I'm storming back to the safety of our little bedroom. That's all I do anymore: dig myself further into the hole of flirting and leading on the Prince and then pout about my day's deeds in the bedchambers.

But after tonight, the pouting might be real tears. Real torment and real pain.

My boots pound over the black-bricked sidewalk, through the side entrance of the castle, and the echo of my anxious steps follows after me as I stride down the dark hall and slip into the safe haven of the last door hidden in the corner of the castle.

My bedroom—I mean, *their* bedroom.

A pressing breath shoves out at that thought too. This

isn't my home. Someday I'll find my place in the world, but first I have to help these men.

No matter what it costs.

I tell myself that over and over again as I slip beneath the blankets. I snuggle down so deep the warm blanket covers my head, and I just soak in the comfort of the silence.

"Cersia," someone says, stomping all over that sweet silence.

My lashes lift slowly to the darkness beneath my den of covers.

"Yes?" I have to put real effort into not growling out that little word.

The bed dips. My weight jostles. A hard chest presses against my private cocoon. I don't dare move though.

Maybe—just maybe—if I stay still enough, he'll go away. He'll get the hint of the burial-like blankets I've submerged myself in, and he will surely go away.

"Cersia, I think we should talk," Avian says, clearly not understanding my hints.

I really did think he was the smart one too.

A sigh leaves my lips, and I close my eyes once more.

I don't have the energy today.

The blanket remains over my face, but I listen to his sweet words. I couldn't ignore him if I wanted to.

"You know you don't have to move this fast? It's barely been a week, just take your time. Earn his trust slowly... I-I—"

Whatever sentiment was on the tip of his tongue, it's pushed aside as the bedroom door bangs shut and another bossy male stomps all over my private little quietness.

"I canceled your night with the Prince," Roman announces, his voice hard with assertive sureness.

At that sudden statement, I fling the blankets down and sit up with ramrod straight posture. "You did what?!" I can't keep the annoyance from grating my tone.

"I told him you weren't feeling well." Roman lifts his bronze shoulders with a careless shrug that I want to shake right out of him.

My legs tangle with Avian's as I climb on top of him, his silver eyes wide with stunned surprise. *Surprise, bitch, I'm gonna kill your friend right in front of you.*

I shove off of him, and my bare feet slam over each board as I bring myself inches from this little empty skulled man. "You fucked up my plans? You canceled the date I worked days to get?" My anger flares hot between us, and his pretty eyes darken as he looks down the straight line of his nose to glare properly at me.

"I saved you. I. *Saved*. You. You can say thank you now."

"Thank you?!" My voice shakes so hard I nearly choke on it.

"Yeah. You're fuckin' welcome."

Oh no, he didn't.

My palms land on the smooth panes of his chest, and I shove him with all the strength I possess. He stumbles back, but he recovers fast, and he reacts even faster.

Strong arms wrap around me like a vise, and my hair flings over my face as he spins me until my back is against his front. He holds my arms crisscrossed against my breasts, and I'm seething from the manhandling he seems to think he's entitled to do.

Why do they hold me like this? All of them constantly spin me around like a princess, just wrap me into submission.

My foot lifts, but I quickly realize he's wearing boots, and the pain there won't be enough.

So my head flings back in the matter of half a second. Pain sears through my skull as I crack that blow against his perfect little nose.

"Fucckk," he hisses like a sweet secret against the back of my neck. "Why do you hate my nose? Why? Fuck, Cersia!"

Fuck indeed.

"Okay, let's calm down." Avian stands, and though Roman is still cursing, he hasn't released me yet either.

Impressive.

"She's right," Avian draws every ounce of my attention, and I look up at him through a tangle of hair hanging in my face. "Don't put yourself in the Prince's way again, Rome." The intensity in the shifter's gaze is as daunting as it is worried.

He's worried about me as well as Roman.

"You can't protect everyone, Av," Roman grinds those words out, his hold on me wrapping around me in more of a touch of comfort rather than aggression.

Is he...is he hugging me right now?

What. The. Fuck.

"And if you don't watch your step, you'll be as cursed as the witch." The ominous darkness that clings to Avian's low-spoken warning crawls over my skin.

"The Night Witch is cursed?" It doesn't occur to me that I'm still having this conversation while Roman snuggles me from behind like I'm the slut puppy's favorite chew toy.

"She's...exiled from hell." Avian looks from Roman to me and then back again, and I can tell there's so much more they can't say. "That's not the point. The point is, Roman's going to stop playing hero before he gets his throat slit."

"He wouldn't kill me. He enjoys watching me suffer. But he'd gladly have you kill me just to watch you suffer. You gonna do that for your Prince? You gonna take my life?" Roman snaps back with cruelty cutting into his every word.

A scent of rage stings the air, and in a flash of dark magic, Avian's chest collides with mine. His hand reaches high, and he grips the other man's neck so fast I don't realize what's happened until Roman and myself are both pinned against the wall.

"Don't talk to me like you talk to them. Don't parade around your little *I don't give a fuck* attitude like you do for the rest of this kingdom." Avian seethes the words out with his face just inches from mine, his anger breathing down Roman's throat.

While I stand between the two men and try not to make a sound.

But I can't help it.

I can't fucking help the gasp that slides from my lips.

Because during the heat of their threats, both of the cocks grow hard against me. Roman's presses along the curve of my ass while Avian's thickness grinds into my stomach.

And yet neither of them acknowledges the lust I feel washing through all three of us with me at the center of it all like a boat caught within the reckless waves of a riptide. Drown me in these waters. Let me die here in the rushing current of these beautiful emotions.

Avian senses it first. I don't know how. I'll never understand his intuition.

His lips part, and then his head dips down, and he's focused on me. His hand that's not around Roman's neck drops to my hip. A line forms between his dark brows as he seems to consider the way my skin feels beneath the back and forth drifting of his thumb.

Is he testing himself? Testing me? Or is he...trying to make some kind of decision?

Whatever it is, his mind seems to decide sooner rather than later.

Ever so slowly, he leans closer. His nose skims along mine as the warmth of his breath sears over my lips, and I breathe him in like all I want is a single taste. Our gazes lock. Our lips nearly brush. Our hearts pound as one.

And then he pauses.

He's going to back away.

He's going to run out of this room and away from me like they do time and time again.

Then he closes his eyes. And he presses his lips to mine with the sweetness he instills with every word he ever speaks. It's a gentle caress of his mouth along mine. A fleeting soft kiss with more emotion than I've felt in all my life pressed into a span of less than a single minute.

He pulls away from me, but the space he allows between us is very little. His gaze lingers along my lips even though he cannot see them. And it's then that his palm lifts, his fingertips skim the edge of my jaw, and he touches my features for the very first time.

I close my eyes just as I had when he kissed me. Somehow this feels wildly more intimate. It's the lightest touch along my neck, my jaw, my lower lip and the bow just above. As if I'm a fragile, delicate flower, he brushes over the lines of my face. My lashes flutter as he takes me in little by little with a caress that makes me weak in the knees.

When he reaches my hair and his fingers slide in, he stops there.

He doesn't look back up at me. He blinks over and over again as he looks down at the small space between us.

"The most beautifully pained woman in all the realms," he whispers like an echo.

My heart pounds for more. I don't know why.

I know I'm pretty.

But I need his response to that beauty. Did it live up? Were my looks something that was talked too highly of, and now after all this time, does it live up to the name of most beautiful woman in all the realms?

I cling to his silence.

His head lifts slowly. His lips hover over mine. And then he finally speaks. "The Goddess did bless you. With a beautiful, resilient soul that shines through without even looking at you, Cersia."

My heart. My poor, poor stupid heart. It skips and flops and falls right out of my chest, I swear it.

When his lips find mine once more, it's a demanding passion. His tongue slides over mine before our lips ever fully seal. He devours me, and the hold he has on my hair tightens just as the hold Roman has against my torso pulls harder against himself. The press of their bodies against mine drills untamed desire all through me.

And it seems I'm not the only one.

Fingers grip my chin harshly, and I'm pulled away from that addicting kiss with a gasp slipping from my lungs. But I never catch that breath.

Because Roman pulls my mouth right to his, and he tastes me slowly. He runs the tip of his tongue over my damp lower lips, and I can't decide if he wants my kiss... or Avian's. It doesn't matter, and he doesn't seem to let the thought linger. His dominance is all he shows me as he thrusts his tongue into my mouth and gives me the slowest, deepest exploration. He takes every part of me, and the slower he moves his mouth against mine, the slower he starts to thrust his hips against the curve of my ass.

And that's what sets us all off. Avian grips my thighs and hoists me higher until I'm lined up with the hardest part of him. I'm twisted one way to kiss Roman while Avian controls my sex against his cock with hard grinding thrusts that just distract me from that delicious thing Roman keeps doing with his tongue.

It isn't competitive. Jealousy doesn't exist here. It's the sharing of emotions. We all want the same thing. They prove that even more when I pull back from Roman's mouth, and he doesn't pause for a second as Avian slams his lips against his friend's.

Their kiss is harsher. It's like seeing an ember burn for so long that the heat is unbearable when it finally ignites. There's a desperateness in the flick of their tongues, the biting of lips, the growling of pleasure.

And I feel every bit of that desperation as each of them slides their hands down the front of my pants at the same time, snapping the button right off the front as they both push their fingers over every inch of my sex. My thighs clench around Avian's lean hips just as a cutting gasp tears from my lungs, and one of them sinks in hard while the other presses slow teasing circles over the most sensitive part of me.

"I-I um..." What. Are. Words.

They don't exist. Only shaking gasps of air manage to fall from my parted lips, and even those aren't really sure of how my lungs are actually supposed to function.

"What is it, beautiful?" Roman's tone has that taunting sentiment, but it's different right now. Sensual with smooth but gravelly whispers.

"I—" Fuck. What...? "I-I think we should move to the bed," I finally manage to stutter out.

Avian only hums along my throat as he nips there with sharp teeth and a soothing tongue.

"No. No, I think right here is fine," Roman says hotly against the shell of my ear, his fingers thrusting in and rubbing along a spot he seems to be rather fond of.

I am too, it seems. The moan he works out of me is like the one thing he seems to want in life, because I feel his smile curve against his lips as he kisses along my jaw and massages deeper, harder, faster.

Roman's big hand holds me steady, and I can't even focus on either man as trembles start to shake through my core. My jeans are pulled away. Cold air meets my skin, but then...warm air is along my thighs. My feet plant against hard shoulders, and the heat of steady exhales washes over the apex of my thigh. Lips skim with a hint of pressure there. Roman continues to pump into me with his palm slapping on the verge of pain and pleasure.

Until a warm mouth slides over his fingers, over my sex and consumes both of us with the swirl of his tongue. The gasp that trembles out of me is nearly a scream. Hard pressure flicks over my clit. Again. And again. And again before he sucks so hard there at the same time as Roman rocks right into that spot deep inside me.

Then I'm soaking down his hand, my palm finding

his shoulder behind me, and I cling to him desperately as every part of me trembles against him. Echoes of my pleasure climb the walls and cascade around us.

Avian's demanding tongue never does stop.

And neither does my release.

It comes again and again, slamming, pounding, consuming me entirely.

I'm a wreck. I don't even know how they're keeping me from sliding to the floor into a pile of useless arms and legs that no longer possess the ability to work anymore.

Their torturous movement against my wetness halts after a lifetime of pleasure passes me by. A tattered breath finds my lungs, and I almost remember that I should continue doing that. Breathing is good.

Yes. Yes.

My head falls back, and I focus on the weak inhales and exhales. The sweetness of his words wash over my neck as he takes me in like my pleasure is his own.

"Now we can go to the bed," Roman says like sex and secrets.

My eyebrows arch high.

Because we're just beginning, it seems.

And I have no idea how I'm going to keep up with two of them.

Avian pulls me close until my knees bend over his shoulders, his big hands wrap around the small of my stomach, and then he hauls me up. My hands grapple to hold on to his neck as a smile plays adorably against his lips, and he walks me across the room like that, as if he's not even close to being done with his time between my thighs.

I pray to the Goddess that he lives there forever.

He smiles so hard at me that a charming dimple appears in his left cheek, and my hand relaxes just enough for my thumb to sweep up and trace that sexy feature near his full lips. His silver eyes are locked on me as he tilts his head and brushes his mouth slowly over the inside of my wrist.

Then he drops me, hands held out at his sides as I free fall down with an unattractive yelp crawling up my throat. My ass bounces against the bed, and I lie there for a moment, staring up at two devilish men smirking down on me.

Avian steps slightly closer as I'm spread out before him. As for Roman, he's slowly unbuckling his pants, his penetrating gaze never leaving mine the entire time he unbuttons, hooks his thumbs, and then shoves off the last stitch of formality that was between us.

There's nothing formal about him and me now. My wetness is bared to them both. And Roman's cock is so hard it wavers, catching my attention and bringing an ache to my core that I had previously thought they'd soothed.

Not enough, it seems.

"Take your shirt off," Roman whispers through a growl, his pale eyes shining in the dim lighting with sinister, sensuous intent.

Several hard beats of my heart pass as I blink up at

him before my brain kicks in and I scramble to do exactly as he says. Not only that, but my thoughts go into overdrive, and I take his demanding words and practically echo them right back.

"Take your pants off," I command of Avian in a loud voice that's a little too desperate to be ladylike.

Fuck ladylike. Ladylike doesn't exist here. I'll save that etiquette for when I'm not still dripping wet from an orgasm two men happily gave me.

Avian's slow demeanor is so much more confident and fluid than my flailing undressing. His boyish smile is sexy, and his big hands work below his waist to slide off his pants in a casual display of certainty.

Is he that certain in all aspects of his life? Will he be that confident in just a little while?

Because now, we're naked.

And my slamming heart is all too aware of what might come next.

"You're anxious. You're never anxious..." Roman tilts his head at me with a gentleness smoothing his sharp features. "Come here, beautiful."

I lift until I'm on my knees, and my hands find the soft blanket as I crawl to him with my ass swaying just slightly. His dark eyebrows shift higher and that smile on his lips turns devious.

"Not too anxious, it seems," Avian says, and I have absolutely no idea how he knows what I'm doing, but the way he bites back his smirk tells me he's very aware.

"I'm not. I'm not nervous." I peer up at one man and

then the other from beneath my thick lashes. I'm aware of my body. I'm aware of my beauty. I'm assured in both. But the dynamics of the three of us are not something I've ever considered.

I want—I want to make them feel as safe and happy and so, so fucking good as they make me feel.

Part of me is terrified this could all easily go wrong, and once it goes wrong, nothing will be the same.

So right now, I have to make sure tonight goes so very right.

I hold the smoldering look in Roman's eyes as my head lowers down the hard panes of his body. My tongue sweeps along the lines there, trailing down, down, down. I don't look away from him until the smooth tip of his cock kisses my lips, and my mouth opens to take his rigid shaft as deep as my throat will let me. My hand against his hip steadies the bobbing of my head, and despite the sexy groan he releases, it's not enough.

It never will be.

Not when we're like this.

My other hand reaches, and I feel Avian's hard muscles beneath my fingertip. With a jerk of his hip, I bring him closer.

Closer.

And closer.

And closer.

Until he's just near enough...for their tips to touch, and my tongue to swirl over one, and then the other.

The whispered groan of curses surprises me when I

realize it's Avian worshiping the word *fuck* again and again. I slide down his shaft and then his friend's just to do it all over again simply because I like the way those nasty words sound against his tongue. Avian's hand sinks through my hair, and it's Roman's cock he shoves me down deeper against like he wants to imprint the image of my mouth fucking his best friend.

The idea of that alone is what pulses want through the sensitive spot just between my thighs.

And as if he senses that too, Avian pulls my hair hard and doesn't stop until I'm looking up at him with hooded eyes and gasping lips.

"Come here," Avian rasps, taking a seat at my side, spreading his legs wide and not waiting a single second for me to comply. He drags me roughly by the hair right where he wants me. My legs straddle his, but he tilts my head back harder just to kiss up the column of my throat and along my ear.

"You're so fucking beautiful in ways you'll never understand, Cers." He whispers that sentiment and it's tinged with sweet aggression. The possessiveness of his words shivers over my skin. The mixture of kindness and control in his tone is a form of lust I've never heard before.

His rough palms skim over my hips, and he lifts me, my chest brushing over his slowly as he slips his tongue along my neck in a form of distracting delicious kisses. He sucks and bites and caresses my skin, and my hands meet his strong shoulders as he lowers me ever so slowly back down his chest.

His tip slides over my wetness and pulls a cutting sigh from my lungs as his hardness grinds against my clit just right. He takes his time teasing there as if it's just to hear me breathe my approval out on shaking gasps and groans.

Another set of warm hands trail down my sides, over my breasts and along my ribs before gripping my hips and shoving me down hard in one fast move. Avian's thickness slams in, and the soundless pleasure against my lips turns to a long scream I can't contain.

"Mmm, he feels good, huh, beautiful?" Roman murmurs like a prayer. "You like both of us taking care of your sweet fucking pussy, don't you?" His hold on me becomes tighter as his nails dig into my flesh, and he guides my hips faster against this friend. "Let me take care of you. Let me take care of both of you," he says in the quietest lust-filled whisper.

The pace he instills in me slows. He almost has me stop entirely, and I'm not complaining as I try to find the breath lost in my lungs. I start to wonder what he's doing even as a beat slips by. But then his fingers blaze down my spine, slowly trailing lower and lower. Then he presses hard on the small of my back and arches my ass against his hardness. A tremble wrecks through me, but I trust him. I trust both of them.

Avian's intuition, his sex sense or whatever it is, picks up on the small change of my hips even as he still fills me completely. His mouth presses to my throat once more before he slams his lips hard against mine, slips his tongue along mine and distracts me as much as he seems to be distracting himself.

But why?

What does he think is going to hap—

A hard press of smooth rigidness slides between my thighs and against my opening. My muscles tighten. Avian rocks his hips slowly against mine, and Roman just soaks up the feel of his friend fucking me by sliding his shaft back and forth there along the base of Avian's cock.

My lashes flutter, but I focus on the kiss. I focus on the flick of his tongue and the caress of his mouth against mine. I kiss Avian so intently that I no longer tense when Roman slides against my pussy once more. Even as he slides right into the tightness of my walls.

A moan pulls from deep inside me, and Avian consumes the sound of that pleasure with a deepening kiss. Roman's groan hums against the back of my neck, and it only grows louder as he fucks me deeper and fucks Avian harder. A reckless moan cuts from Avian's lips as his friend slides harder and harder against his cock that's filling me intensely. Having both of them is a filling feeling that verges on pain and pleasure. It's like I can't catch up. Like my body doesn't know how to handle them both, my lungs lose air, my heart misses beats, and my mind...it's lost in euphoric bliss.

The arch of my back is the only thing keeping me held together as Roman's pace quickens and Avian continues to devour my mouth. It's dirty, nasty fucking during sweet, caressing kissing.

My heart can't take it.

And neither can my body.

The release that shatters through my core spirals over every single nerve ending in my body until I'm screaming into the now starry-filled room that I can't focus on to save my life. All I know is the sensation of tingling numbness that pricks at my skin. I'm lost in that feeling.

It doesn't fade away until the pulsing feel of Avian's cock deep inside me demands my attention as his breath shakes against mine on a growling groan that meets my tongue. His palms grip me harder, and I let him use me to hold himself together. My fingers sink through his hair, and he falls apart in my hands.

But Roman never stops. And the shaking of my body begins all over again. I try to delay it. I try to ride out the slamming feel of his body thrusting against mine harder and harder, but it's all too much. The emotions are too high.

The orgasm that he demands from me is a tightening thing as it releases me but clenches him. And that alone seems to be what gives him what he needs. I can't think about what my body is giving him, but he takes it all the same.

And I'd give him even more if I could.

...I'd give these men everything.

It's a terrifying thought that slips through my mind as our bodies slow but our hearts continue to soar. I wonder if they sense that heart-pounding fear that's inside my soul all because I let myself care about these men who stormed into my life.

I don't care. I'll embrace that fear.

Eventually.

Roman slips from me but lingers there with his hands intimately wrapped around me from behind just as Avian lowers his head to my chest, and the three of us just breathe one another in. Our emotions are just as entangled as our bodies. It's the most beautiful moment in time.

Until it's not.

"What. The. Literal. Fuck," Zilo roars before the door even slams closed behind him.

And then the moment is gone.

FOURTEEN

SHIT

Zilo will make a very good disappointed father someday.

I know this by how fast he threw my clothes at me, pinging me in the head with a boot, and marched me right outside before the sun even warmed the horizon, ranting through his teeth the entire time.

"*Find the most beautiful woman in all the realms,* the fucking witch said. *She'll solve all our problems,* the fucking witch said." The man I had previously thought was a total alpha fuck is currently waving his arms around dramatically like a pack of women during a gossip fest.

I don't say a word as he leads us a mile away from the dark castle to just behind a large barn-like structure that smells slightly like burning demonic pig shit. He stops abruptly at a large divot, and in the dim morning sunlight, I can almost make out that it's a pond of sorts.

"You have to get the scent off." Zilo rubs his enormous hand down his face in the slowest possible look of frustration.

My lip curls as I peer down at the muddy ravine before me. This is how they problem solve? This is really the only solution to scent masking?

"Avian and Roman don't have to do this?" The two assholes stand in silence behind their alpha-hole leader, looking like they couldn't even possibly know me let alone have fucked me an hour ago.

The fuckers.

Literally.

"Avian and Roman know how to shift. Your beast has its own primitive smell. Once you shift, you smell like beast. Shift. It's that easy." Zilo blinks at me like he expects a magic trick to be revealed.

Honestly in this moment, if I could pull a rabbit out of my vagina and call it my beast, I would.

"I fucking can't."

"Then. Get. In. The. Mud." His head bobs obnoxiously.

I swallow hard. "No."

His dark brows bounce.

"No?"

"Nnnooo," I repeat slowly for his little puppy brain to follow along.

I note the quiet look Avian passes Roman, but still they stand back as if they have nothing to do with this fucktacular position I'm in.

They were a bit more supportive when they were happily bending me in those other positions earlier though, weren't they?

My eyes roll hard.

Zilo's shoulders square at the same time as his hands grip his hips, and he gives me a stern glaring at.

That'll teach me.

Goddess, he's such a fuc—

My feet are off the ground with a smoky puff of magic and a grunt of noise from the asshole hauling me over his shoulder and plowing me toward the ground. My nails dig into his back, his shoulders, his ass, anything to help me from smacking the hard earth.

But I never do. He keeps hold of me as we both slosh into the swamp-like mud. It's—It's not even mud. It's thin like water, but clumpy with...

"Is this shit?"

"I mean...only a little," Roman whispers so quietly I barely hear him.

"Oh. My. Fucking. Sanity." I stiffen in Zilo's arms as he lowers me down against him, his chest sliding disgustingly against mine.

"It's good for you. Covers the smell." A hint of a smile plays at the corner of Zilo's lips, his dark beard and hair making him look devilishly handsome as he stares down at me.

"Yeah. Because I smell like shit now!"

His big hand lifts with a slurp, and he lazily rakes his palm down the side of my face. The grime of it rolls between his fingertips and my skin, and a gasping shriek escapes my mouth. Wide-eyed and fuming, I bore a hole through the center of his damn face. There's a good three seconds where I can't even fathom how to react.

What's the protocol when the guy you have a sweet love-hate relationship with wipes feces across your face?

I lift my hands to either side of his jaw, and he simply holds my gaze like he doesn't believe a single word I haven't even spoken yet.

"Don't do it, Cersia." His tone is all gravelly threat, but he doesn't have the shifter balls to back it up.

"Do what, Zilo?" My hands clap against his gruff beard, and his smile only widens as he closes his eyes and takes what he deserves.

Even as I slowly shove my fingers through his long black hair and braids.

"There's something seriously wrong with him right now." Roman's words distract me only slightly.

Because he's right...Zilo isn't angry.

I'm covering his handsome face in literal shit, and he's...smiling.

"There's definitely something wrong with him," Avian agrees.

My heart beats a little harder, a little more recklessly as I stare up at him with his lashes closed, his face smooth without those hard lines of frustration creasing his features. He's beautiful.

"Happy?" he asks flatly.

"Immensely." And I can't help but smile. The

pleased feeling of getting him back mixed with the warming sensation of seeing him so raw and beautiful right now, I can do nothing but smile.

Until he dunks me entirely.

When I surface, muddy shit flings through the air as I awkwardly gasp for a clean breath. And still he smiles. The audacity of this furry fuck! How dare he!

I'm going to kill him. I will. I'll murder him and bury him in a shit shallow grave right here. I'm going to—

His smile disappears as he stares down at me, and a somber look in his eyes sinks right through my chest with heavy dread that feels like it's more his than my own.

"What's wrong?" I can't help but ask.

His Adam's apple bobs as he takes his time answering me.

"The Prince requested to see you this morning. First thing." The words sound like a death sentence in the quietness of his hard tone.

A prickling uneasiness crawls over my muddy flesh.

Because Prince Ravar only wants one thing in the mornings.

And today, it's me.

FIFTEEN

A LOSING WINNER

The halls are silent but filled with the pounding of my anxious heart. Everything I've worked for is right in the palms of my hands, and I'm now standing before my fate.

The last time I stood outside his room, screams of false pleasure rattled the door. It's quiet now. I hate it. I quickly bathed in the magical bath waters. I'm now spotless. I'm dressed nicely.

But I don't have a real plan ready. I don't know how I can do it.

I won't fuck him. I just won't. But if that's the only way to distract him enough to kill him...

My hair wafts against my back from how hard I shake my head at myself. Nope. Can't do it. Killing him is one thing, sex, that's just asking for too much. Even as a last request.

A deep inhale fills my lungs as I lift my hand to the cold door handle. My eyes close, and I count to three.

One.

Two.

A shiver of crawling fingers grips my shoulder like knives cutting into flesh.

"What are you doing?" Familiar black eyes are wide and devouring as the Night Witch assesses me from head to toe. "And why do you reek of pigs and farm animals?"

Wow. Thanks, Zilo.

"Never mind." Her long glossy black hair skims along her inky lips as she speaks to me in a rush as she always seems to do. "Do not kill him." My mouth opens to interrupt her, but she quickly carries on, peering over her shoulder this way and that as she speaks. "You don't want it done in private. You don't want your friends to take any blame or punishment, correct?" A thin eyebrow lifts expectantly, but as always, she knows the answer to her very own question.

"No."

I try to follow her line of thinking, but this is literally what we've wanted from the start.

"Roman will be the suspect. They will pin it on him in any way they can. The demons of this realm idolize Ravar as one of their own. The hell fae, not so much. And the hellhounds and shifters, they despise him for what he does to his very own High Hell. So do not let there be any backlash toward Roman or your friends. We've worked too hard for this to be a deed done in private." The darkness in her eyes flashes, and my mind reels to find an alternate path that doesn't harm the High Hell or myself.

"The men are planning poison for you to deliver tonight during a special announcement." Once more, I want to ask the details of this special announcement, but she doesn't leave time for minor things like plans or particulars. "But as I said, they'll put themselves in harm's way by doing it in such a mysterious way. Trust me. Everything will be ready tonight. Just...don't get stabby in the meantime."

"What exactly—"

"No. Trust me. Tonight." She nods until I too nod back at her. "No stabby," she echoes with seriousness.

"Okay. No stabby," I repeat, shaking my head at how foolish this conversation suddenly feels. But a half plan is better than no plan. And that's all my men keep leaving me with.

I blink hard, and no matter how long I hesitate, my pounding heart never calms. Finally, I accept it for what it is. This is a real goal and an almost plan. *Tonight*. I'll be ready.

When I look up to tell her just that, no one's there. Dense darkness and eerie silence are all that she leaves me with in the empty hall.

The cry of a slow pulling hinge tears me away from searching the vacancy, and when I turn toward the sound of it, the Prince is already striding out to me. His palms push down my sides like I'm his favorite blanket he's ready to wrap himself up in. His head dips low, and he nuzzles my neck with his lips already parted and his tongue ready to strike. But at the very last second, he pulls ever so slowly away, his lips curling back strangely with a questioning confusion lining his face.

Shit! I still smell like shit!

Thank the Goddess I fucking smell like flaming pig shit!

"You, um, you look delicious this morning," he says stiffly but politely as he detangles himself from my apparent repulsive embrace.

Just to really solidify my disgusting unfuckable status a little more, I fluff my hair with a dramatic toss of my hand. "Thank you, my Prince."

He audibly gags.

Zilo, I fucking love you. I take back every cruel thing I've ever thought about you.

Well, most of it.

I lift my hand to his sharp jawline, and my index finger barely makes sexy contact before he dips and dives away from my touch.

"I—" His throat clears harshly, almost like he's fighting the urge to breathe regularly. "I have a gift for you, my lovely."

I halt the funny business, and my hand drops to my side immediately.

A gift?

The Prince of Hell got me a gift...that's...sweet. I guess.

I almost feel bad for leading him on. And yeah, the whole plotting his death stuff too.

"I'd like to make a special announcement tonight," he

says, and I nod quietly as if this is the first I'm hearing of the mysterious announcement. "After the announcement, I'd like to give you a very special gift to tell you how much you mean to me."

The announcement. He's going to announce that I'm his new bride of the century!

Confetti shoots off in my mind, and I just want to rub it in Roman's face that I didn't lose after all. I won.

And tonight, Prince Ravar will announce it. And then, I'll fucking kill him to celebrate.

"You're too generous, my Prince," I coo.

"And you're too salacious." He takes a step toward me like he just can't help himself.

But.

It seems he can.

His throat bobs, and he stifles a breath and a noise in his throat that sounds like barely contained vomit.

"Tonight," he confirms as he takes a step back. "I wanted to have a talk with you first," he declares, motioning toward his room, and at this point I am very assured he's no longer thinking about sex. He may never think about sex with me ever again.

As it should be.

I smile sweetly and sway my hips this way and that to really stir up that pheromone smell the boys were ranting and raving about not so long ago.

The Prince's bedroom consists of one thing and one thing only. An enormous circular bed with black satin sheets perfectly fitted across the fluffy mattress.

No quilts but endless pillows adorn the bed. This space isn't for sleeping, clearly.

Not one chair can be found in the spacious room. A fireplace flames with heat from the wall directly across from the bed, but other than that, there's nothing else to see here.

I make myself at home and sit comfortably on the plush mattress.

He winces.

Oh, I am just killing him right now.

Just to really—literally—rub it in, I fall back against the smooth sheets and stare up at his glittering black ceiling.

"You wanted to talk?" I ask in a sultry voice.

"Yes," he coughs, and I'm very aware of how much space he's keeping between us.

I roll over and keep going until I pop back up and face him, my scent almost getting the best of me in this moment, but I'm too good to gag at my own smells.

At least...I think I am. My stomach turns, but I swallow the thick, sickly sensation down.

"I wanted to know about your life. Your family are white wolves?" His hand half covers his mouth in a less than discreet appearance of subtlety.

"Yes. From the upper realm. I lived in a quiet forest south of the Kingdom of Borne." I keep the pretty smile in place, but I'm suddenly aware of how careful I should tread. I haven't won yet. And now he's quizzing me rather than eating up the pretty words I always feed him.

"What does your beast look like, Cersia? Is she as beautiful as you? Does she have an angry streak in her?" The depths of his inky gaze are intently held on me, and I shift as I cross my legs casually.

"I-I don't know really. My father died years ago, and I never learned to use that side of myself." It's the truth. Mostly.

"Because...you're afraid or because someone didn't want you to?"

My lips part, and I don't really want to admit to either, but one of those two truths is safer than the other.

"I suppose I am afraid." The weak wane of my smile is honest.

I hate how real those words are. But admitting that my father feared for me to reveal the beast inside myself, that's too much to tell anyone.

I'll die with that secret.

"But you're not a hell fae?" he asks oddly.

A hell fae?

"Why would you think that, my Prince?"

"Answer the question, Cersia." His lips are a thin crack against his serious face.

"No. I'm not any sort of fae."

Pure relief smooths the tension in his features.

"They're more shifting than any shifter I've ever met. More demonic than any demon. Their glamours are forbidden, and some of their own kind have been exiled from my kingdom. They're lucky they're not slaughtered into extinction like the dragons once were so long ago. I appreciate your beauty, but do not ever lie to me. Because I won't hesitate to slit your pretty throat, Cersia." A manic glint shines in his eyes, and it's held on me for so long I become all too aware of my beating heart.

"I would never, my Prince," I say with a tilt of my chin lifting high to show him as much respect as I've ever given anyone.

And it's a fucking lie. I cling to that lie like it'll save my life.

Indeed, I hope it does.

"You're dismissed," he says flatly with a sudden snapping click of his fingers. He does it three times.

It startles me until I realize it's a doggy order that Avian hasn't yet taught me.

I refrain from rolling my eyes or doing anything more than shuffle across the room with too many emotions churning through my stomach.

My gaze is lowered to the floor as I pass him by, and he moves clear out of my way as I pass. There's no longer humor in the shitty antics anymore though.

Not a single ounce of happiness is in me.

Because I entered this room feeling like I'd won the game.

And now I'm not so sure if I'll even survive it.

SIXTEEN

THE TIME HAS COME

When I return to the safe haven of their bedroom, there's a long white gown hanging near the bath. It's thin and sheer like my one from home, but black glittering diamonds are gleaming along the hem of the sleeves and the base of the dress.

It's a gift. Just like he said he had a gift for me.

I hate how much it looks like a mating gown.

I ran away from one of those already.

At least that ceremony wasn't going to end in my death.

What if he knows why I was truly brought here? What if he knows about my affiliation with the exiled witch? What if he kills me before I kill him?

"You're going to be his bride!" Zilo says happily with a big clap of his hands as he walks in behind me followed by two more less than excited hellhounds.

"You should tell her the plan," Avian says suddenly.

The smile shining in his friend's eyes drains away rather quickly. "No. It'll put her in danger." Zilo skims past me and takes a seat on the settee, making it seem tiny beneath his enormous frame. His legs spread wide as he makes himself comfortable, but he doesn't look at all comfy really.

He's tense. The hard lines of his shoulders and chest are deep cutting.

But I can't focus on any of them.

"I know the plan," I whisper.

Roman's dark eyebrows slowly rise, but he says nothing. No one does. They're too afraid of repeating their plans, and I'm too exhausted to even have this conversation. There's a weight on my shoulders that's grown real over the last several minutes.

I came here for a reason. And now the time has come.

"I have to get ready," I tell them, and the tragic emptiness in Avian's eyes isn't from his blindness at all. It's like he wants to steal me away from all the things he's thrown me into.

It's too late for that.

"Yeah," Zilo agrees with an uncertain nod of his head. He might be uncertain, but I know he'll fake his confidence until the day he dies. "Yeah. And...take a bath. I could smell you all the way down the hall."

Great.

Good talk, Zilo.

Roman and Avian are still staring at me, and it isn't until Zilo nudges them one after the other that they follow him out. A sort of aching pain pulses through my heart with the sound of the door clicking closed behind them.

I stand in a daze long after they're gone. My body goes through the motions of a life worth living. Of a future Princess in the making.

I bathe. I comb my long blonde hair. I slide into the sleek dress my Prince gifted me. I glance only once at the beautiful, blue-eyed woman staring wide-eyed at me in the reflection of the inky bathwater.

And then I know I'm ready.

I'm going to kill my future mate.

The dinner that evening is finer than I've seen in this hellish realm. The meat is tender and seasoned, and some of the patrons even have the decency to use utensils from time to time. I spy Zilo and Avian holding the food in their hands, and a small smile almost pulls at my lips.

I suppose you can't always teach old dogs new tricks.

The Prince's hold on my hip tightens, and when I gaze up at him, he's watching me closely. I'm seated on his lap as his legs dangle over the ledge of his favorite little perch. We're sitting high above hundreds of tables. A quiet chatter of his people enjoying a delicious meal scuttles below us.

And he's watching me with piercing dark eyes.

"What are you looking at, my lovely?" he asks,

wafting hot air against my ear in a clammy uncomfortable sensation.

"Nothing," I whisper along his neck, teasing his flesh while distracting his mind.

If he thinks too hard on the way I look at his High Hell, would he kill them?

Would he kill me?

A clatter of fine china clinks against the table set behind us, and from over Ravar's shoulder, I lock eyes with the pale irises of the next heir to the throne.

"Thank you, brother," the Prince drones without looking back at Roman. "Leave us."

A single heartbeat passes by before his voice raises and startles a gasp from my lungs. "I said, get! I took the honor of your braids the last time you lingered too long with a bride of mine. Don't make me take the honor of your manhood next," Ravar grumbles as he gazes cruelly out at the crowd.

My mouth can't seem to close.

He took...he took away his brother's most prideful possession? He took away his honor?

Why?

Roman's attention never leaves me, and there's a desperate look in his pretty gaze. Very distinctly, his index finger lingers on the glass to the right. His brow lifts.

Ever so subtly, I nod.

Leave. Just go before the Prince's maliciousness creeps out again.

Roman turns with his scarred back lined with tension. And my attention finally falls to the wine glass.

Poison. That's the best they can do?

Rather unclever really.

But what is my alternative?

Shoving this man to his death right here, right now?

No. He's quick. He'd land on his feet like a vengeful cat filled with grace and toxic entitlement.

I can do better.

My mind circles as I think it all through, and as I do, I notice how close the hell fae are seated tonight. They don't dine in a class of their own nearest the High Hell as they usually do. The several hundred of the dark horned creatures are directly below us.

None of them say a word.

My gaze shifts from one table to the next, and everyone seems alight with happiness as they chew merrily and drink heartily to the special occasion. Except for those deadly dark eyes that peer up at myself and the Prince every few seconds that pass by.

It's a chill of anticipation to have them watch me when I already feel so watched by the man holding me tightly.

"The Night Witch has broken our wards," he says to me on an empty whisper.

His face is vacant, but there's so much thought behind his inky eyes.

"The Night Witch?" I ask with as much confusion as I can muster.

He nods.

"Why do we hate her, my Prince?" I force my fingers to remain steady as I push back the silky black locks from his face.

"I don't," he tells me with an exhale that carries oh so much weight with it. "I love her," he rasps on a broken whisper.

Now the confusion is real.

"She was my soulmate. She was my one and only. I married into the crown. She was queen of this realm. But the magic here can be consuming. It's too much for some people." My heart pounds in rhythm to the heaviness of his every word. "It turned her into beautiful madness. She was pretty like you." He glances my way, and I can't even fathom how the darkness of the Night Witch and myself could ever be compared. "This morning after you left my rooms, a guard told me he spotted Creatchin in the halls for the first time in centuries. The cursed magic in her blood seems to have tainted her physically, but my man said he'd recognize her anywhere. He saw her. He saw her talking to you."

My stomach drops.

My fingers dig into his shoulder instinctively, and it suddenly isn't a question of whether I could shove this man from his ledge but...if he'd do the same to me.

"That was the Night Witch?" I ask in an even tone as I bite back every urge to look for Zilo.

His searching gaze picks apart every detail I give him. And fuck, I hope I give him what he wants to see.

The hold he has against my hip loosens little by little. Seconds slip by. My heart counts each and every moment that it continues to give me life.

"My Prince," Zilo says from somewhere behind Ravar.

I don't dare look away. If I glance away for a single second, it could cost me my life.

"My Prince, the gift you ordered has just arrived," Zilo's words are pointed and, if I'm not mistaken, a little worrisome.

Worried indeed. I too feel that fear cracking open inside myself.

My beast rumbles to life, but I swallow that reckless feeling right back down.

Everything is fine.

Everything is fine.

Everything—

"Cersia?" A delicate, familiar voice says.

Her tone washes over my name like a river that's worn down a stone for years. In this moment, she's a gentle current of water caught up in a brooding deadly storm.

Because my sister is the kind one.

And she shouldn't be here in the kingdom of hell.

"Nyra." I turn in his arms until her heart-shaped face fills my vision. She's there just behind the small table, and she's looking at me with so much distress in her pretty brown eyes. She looks small here. Fragile. Breakable.

"Why are you here?" I turn to the man I was so afraid of just seconds ago. "Why is she here?" I growl out.

"She is your gift, my lovely," he says with a stabbing hint of viciousness. "Do you want to keep your gift?"

Oh no. No. No. No.

"Of course," I whisper on the stiffest of words.

I have to kill this man. Right now.

I stagger out of his arms, and I'm practically stumbling to embrace my sweet sister—to shield her from the sights of the devilish man behind me. I pull her in hard against me until the golden curls of her hair tickle my nose, and still I hold her tight.

"Why are you here?" I breathe those words out on a breath of anxious terror.

"Please take a seat." Prince Ravar is by her side in a flash of blurring dark colors. Then he pulls out the chair to the right.

And like an obedience-trained puppy, she takes a seat.

Right in front of the glass of poison.

The drilling of my heart is so apparent that a sheen of sweat sticks my hair to the edges of my face.

"What's wrong?" the Prince asks as he holds my chair out for me as well.

Does he know?

It isn't even a question. The question is, how much does he know?

"Nothing." The smile plastered against my face isn't

charming at all. It's tense and vomit-containing. It holds back all the sickly feelings turning in my stomach.

"Then sit down." His smile is no longer carving. It's gone entirely. Vicious rage is in his eyes, his posture, in the very stance he holds.

A blade not at all worthy of a dinner party lines the table on my left-hand side. It's ornate with glittering black gemstones, and it curves up in a hard ark that's intended to maim.

He knows.

He knows everything.

In the midst of my panic, Nyra lifts her glass to her pink lips.

My heart stops.

The noise in the room halts as I watch her with wide eyes and shaking hands. And I use those trembling hands to shove the wine glass from her. It tumbles against the black-clothed table and rains down on the rock beneath our feet. It's a clattering sound of anxiety that matches how I feel entirely.

And now every pair of eyes in this room are staring up at us.

The Prince finds his smile, and he looks out at his people below him. "I present to you my beautiful but inelegant bride," he tells them in a booming voice.

A few shifters chuckle. But most are smart enough to gauge the room.

And the room is fucking edgy, my friends.

"Clap for her!" he roars, his face blooming red within the dim lighting.

Applause erupts all around us, and a quiet sound pulls at my attention. Sobs. Hushed tears fall from Nyra's eyes, and I can't imagine how she must feel.

She wanted a normal life. She didn't want chaotic adventure. She wanted love and babies and...peace.

I'm such a fuck up.

My hand finds hers beneath the table, and I try to focus on her energy. She's my family. She's my blood. She's just like my father.

And I need the one thing my father kept me from all those years.

I need my beast.

My eyes close hard, and I think about all those times that energy rattled awake inside me. I think about the untamed power lying dormant within my soul. I think about my Goddess and how much I need her in this moment.

The table in front of me shakes hard as a fist comes down and cracks the wood just beneath my own hand. My lashes fly up, and I meet the inky depths of his gaze before glancing down at the dagger he holds in his fisted hand.

"I'd like you to brand your belongings, my lovely," he says like a lover's secret.

I blink at him slowly, but I feel the hate radiating off of him.

"What do you mean, my Prince?" The quiver in my voice is very real, and I hate how weak it sounds.

"Your Goddess Moon is important to you. You're a wolf shifter, correct? Not a hell fae?" The skepticism in his tone tells me everything.

His beloved queen was a hell fae. And he thinks I'm just like her. Worse yet, he thinks I'm conspiring with her.

He's not entirely wrong.

Nor is he right.

"I swear it, my Prince. I am not a hell fae." Honesty stings my tone, but still he glares down at me.

"Then brand your belongings with the symbol of your Goddess Moon." His gaze shifts slowly, and then he's looking at my sister. With a jerk of my wrist, he turns over my palm and forces the hilt of the blade into my hand with intent.

"No," I declare so loudly I hear chairs scrape across the floors below.

And I just know it's one or possibly three overbearing men.

I have to protect them, and Nyra, and every one of these people this man is hurting day in and day out.

My fingers slip over the cold jewels along the hilt. Something inside me purrs to life as I hold his gaze. A blaze of power crawls through me. Fiery heat licks at the flesh along my arm, my neck, my face.

And then, I lunge at him. The sweep of my arm and the curve of the weapon is a fluidity of motion that's set to kill. The flash of quickness he puts into shoving away from me is faster than my eyes can see. But it doesn't slow me down.

His body tightens every single muscle, and he's storming toward me just as I'm rushing at him. We meet with a collision of fury. My hand arches back, and he is just too fucking fast.

My wrist is in his fist within the blink of an eye, and he holds me back with a smile cutting across his features.

"My sweet, sexy bride. You're weak," he whispers like a sentiment.

The single word from his lips is enough for the beast inside me to roar awake. Its hostility growls through my entire body, and even the Prince himself seems impressed by the hidden creature within me.

Until my elbow flings forward and slams over the bridge of his nose so hard he doesn't immediately react. Blood spews from his face, and his hand lifts slowly to find that it's his own blood.

Real surprise darkens his face.

"You're a weak bitch," he repeats more violently.

Power shakes through me as vicious teeth extend in my mouth. It's something I've felt a time or two in my life, but I've never welcomed it so much in my entire life. My knees bend, and I'm leaping at him in seconds.

He's just faster.

Strong arms wrap around me. It's a vise of a grip as he twists me until my back is to his front and he's hauling me with him as he brings me to my sister.

Her tears are loud and shaking now. Her pretty face is stained with wet sadness. My beast shrinks back at the mere idea of harming her if it gets too close.

"Carve your fucking moon." He twists my arm until the blade in my hand is so near her soft cheek.

"Fuck you," I grind out, my head flinging back to slam into what I hope is his bloody broken nose.

A roar of anger pulses through his body and my arm as he grips my hand so hard the metal of the weapon cuts into my palm.

"It's her face or your fucking life, Cersia!" He brings the curved edge of the blade harder toward her, and it nicks her flesh just slightly.

A drop of blood stains the dark iron.

I struggle through it all with wide, desperate eyes, but it all happens so fast.

Nyra jerks the weapon from my hand, and in a single stroke, she slices the blade from her chin to the corner of her brow.

The scream that cuts from her lungs cleaves through my own chest.

"Nyra." I'm gasping out her name as I kick and beat against the arms that hold me. All I see is her blood, and all I hear is her hurt. "Nyra!" I'm screaming for her, but she isn't aware of me at all as she stares down at the bloody dagger in her unsteady hand.

Ravar is fighting me as I'm fighting him, and it's the most chaotic moment of emotions flooding my mind and soul.

Then a gleam of blackness walks from the shadows. A slender arm reaches forward. Her black nails wrap around the hilt. And in the single blink of an eye, the Night Witch slings the dagger right at me.

It twirls like a dance suspended in time. It's all I see, and I can't think about how she and I got here in this mess of our lives.

But at the last moment, my head turns as far as Ravar's hold on me will let it.

A thudding sound hits hard. I stumble on my feet. The fall to the ground is unsteady and jarring as my skull cracks into the rock.

The Prince's blood soaks over me warmly as he continues to hold me even as the light in his dark eyes fades little by little. His gaze clings to mine, and a whisper is caught in his chest from where the blade is embedded into his heart.

"She—she'll kill you too," he murmurs with a deadly smile.

Those words haunt through my mind as I stare up at the cavernous ceiling above. Applause—real applause—screams through the room as people chant for the queen they lost centuries ago.

The attention of the High Hell look down on me as the three hellacious shifters crowd around me to look for wounds.

There are none physically.

But the cutting smile the Night Witch slices my way, it's deadly indeed.

And the Prince was right.

If I'm not careful, she'll kill me too in the end.

The End.

Thank you so much for reading *The Darkest Wolves*. I have a special place in my soul for asshole shifter men and the snarky women who make them crazy ;)

Book two of Cersia's dark secrets is now available! You can get your copy of *The Sweetest Lies* HERE!

If you want more updates on Cersia and her alpha-holes, deleted scenes, and giveaways, join my Newsletter or Facebook Reader Group!

AK Koonce Newsletter

AK Koonce Reading Between Realms Facebook Group

Need more shifter alpha-holes in your life?
Turn the page to check out AK Koonce's completed series, *To Tame a Shifter*:

TAMING

White flashes of moonlight glint against the glossy surface of the large object in the old mage's palms. Interest fires all through my veins as she lowers it into the dirt, pushing at the dust until it makes a nice mound over the three items. She pats the dirt sweetly once more before turning away, her long dress skimming against the ground as she returns to the dark cottage. Her white hair sways against her back as she leaves, never once looking out at the road where I stand.

I'm a drifter. In a way, I've been a drifter my entire life. In the last five years, I've taken the job pretty seriously though. This small, quiet village within the Kingdom of Minden is nice, unnoticeable, and easy for someone who wants to disappear to do just that.

That's what I love about it.

This mage, Agatha, may be as old and dusty as this village itself, but she's my only friend. I came to check on her. Every few days, I stop by to visit with her and gossip about who the Prince is sleeping with now and why it isn't me. *I'm wasting the beautiful curves of my youth* as she likes to tell me. I don't have the heart to tell the blind woman that the Prince isn't nearly as attractive as she thinks he is.

I might be a little bit of a bitch sometimes, but I'm not about to crush an old woman's fantasies. That's just cruel.

That's what I came here for: mindless chatter. Until Aggie started ominously burying something in her front yard. People only bury things for two reasons: to remember what they once had or to hide what they once had.

The thin material of my dress brushes lightly against my thighs as I quietly make my way up the dirt path. A few overgrown bushes line the front yard, concealing one window and skimming against the glass of the other. Not that she could see me even if she looked out.

But she's a mage. A powerful mage. Much stronger than myself.

If she wanted to know what waited outside her little home, she would.

Hesitantly, I linger near the dirt that's piled over the objects she buried. My gaze shifts to the arched front door. I came here for a visit with a friend.

I don't have many friends. Okay, I don't have any aside from Aggie if I'm being honest. But fuck, she buried something under the light of the full moon. She all but did a ritual out here with a sacrificial goat. She could have disposed of them in a clandestine place, but she didn't. I can't just ignore that.

I lower myself, falling onto my hands and knees, and begin clawing at the dry dirt. It's a rapid and almost manic drive to find out what lies here. My conscience is quickly pushed aside as the dirt sinks into my nails with each handful of earth I rip away. The clinking sound of my bracelets makes my nerves skitter with every sound they make. A smooth curve beneath rocky particles of dirt glides against my fingertips. My palm sweeps over the hard surface once more, pushing aside the grit to see three objects underneath.

They're ...eggs.

Enormous eggs.

Large animals are worth a large price.

The animal trader in me is already mentally calculating what a beast this size could be worth. Imagine what three of them would be valued at.

With both hands, I try to steal away the top one, my arms aching as I realize the monstrous eggs are just as heavy as they look. My gaze flickers back to the golden glow of Agatha's front window. I could come back for the other two, but it's a mile-long walk. Would she come back out tonight?

I pull at the end of my skirt and quickly try to pile the three eggs into the thin material. A tearing sound rips through the silence, but as I stand, they hold in place against my body; straining against the cloth but not falling to the ground.

I'd hate to harm one of them.

I feel like an asshole. Who steals from a blind woman? Who does that?

... I do.

Why would Agatha bury them? She isn't as familiar with creatures as I am. Perhaps she thought they were useless. She's blind, so perhaps she didn't realize they were eggs at all.

But she's also a mage. So it's even more likely she knew what these things were and wanted to rid herself of them as quickly as possible.

I, on the other hand, am not about to throw away money or the lives of whatever these animals may grow up to be.

Their lives will be worth living. I want to make a profit, of course, but honestly, I just can't stand the thought of not helping them. I don't show it, but my little, slightly selfish heart loves these types of mysterious creatures.

Raising and selling magical animals is just a business for me. I can't get attached. I have to make a living in this world the only way I know how.

On awkward steps and with aching arms, I carry the boulder-like eggs home. The dark forest surrounds me, shutting out the majority of the moonlight and making me stumble more than once before my small shack comes into view.

Glowing embers of ruby eyes greet me as I get closer. The sweet little hellhound rubs his warm temple against my thigh as I pass, but I don't have a free arm to return the affection to my pet.

The dark and fuming hellhound, Grim, might just be the love of my life. It's a pathetic love life that I'm leading, I'll admit.

With the force of my hip, I bump open the door. A creaking cry comes from the hinges, and I don't bother closing it behind me as I settle in near the dwindling embers of the fire. The one room home is tiny with a cot on the far left side of the room and a worn and rickety kitchen table on the other side. The small fire easily warms the abandoned shack that I made my home.

The smooth curve of one of the eggs fills my hands. My own reflection peers at me on the iron-like surface. The two others glisten near the fire. In the lighting, I can really make out their details. One's a pure white color. It shimmers like fresh snow, while the one nestled next to it is as dark as blood. The third one, the one that I hold in my hands, is a consuming deep smoky tone.

They're shining and beautiful.

"But what are they?" I whisper to myself.

I have a thing for creatures, the dangerous and the unique, and I've never seen an egg this large. It's even bigger than an ostrich egg. Its structure seems thicker as well. I hold it close to my chest, and my eyes fall closed as a deep breath fills my lungs.

My magic is quiet within me. I've hidden it away and tried to save it up for when I know I'll really need it in the future.

TAMING

It's there though. A numb sort of tingling feeling of power stings through my body.

A blur of a thousand images flickers through my mind. I search past them all until one faded image pulls to the front.

My sight shows me three colossal animals. Their wingspan is the size of the run-down shack that I've called home for the past year. Thick scales cover their bodies like proud armor. Long talons and sharp teeth lash down from the heavens, preparing to scoop up their next prey.

"Dragons." My eyes open once more, the depths of my blue irises are inky in the reflection of its glossy shell.

A strong and quick beat begins to take over my heart.

They're rare.

Deadly.

Expensive.

I've never sold a dragon before. The most I've ever gotten for a magical creature was a year's worth of income for a pegasus. Would have been more if it was a unicorn, but the buyer didn't believe me when I said its horn was just underdeveloped.

A dragon could pay for a new life though. A real life. Imagine how I could live.

With three dragons, I could start over. No longer would I be a drifter running from her past. I could have a home. A family.

A *life*.

A smile pulls at my lips, and I've already made up my mind.

Without another thought, I toss the onyx egg into the fire.

Mages no longer have the darling little reputation that the generations before us had. No, we're feared. My mother hid me away to protect me, but it weakened my powers. When I was older, I studied magic and magical creatures. Studying magical creatures was the safest form of magic I could think of to continue to stay under the radar of those who hunt us. My actual powers grew stronger with the help of Kreedence. I thought he cared about me, but I know now that that was a lie.

My lip curls as I think of the man I thought I loved. I push the thoughts from my mind. It's an old chapter of my life, and I grew from it. I learned more about my trade because of it.

I know creatures from all over the world. It's a specialty of mine.

And I know heat is needed for dragons to survive.

Maybe that's why Agatha disposed of them. Maybe she couldn't get them to hatch.

A cold summer breeze shakes against the worn, open door, threatening to tear it from its weak hinges as it drifts back and forth. The wind catches against my dark hair, but all my focus is on the flames caressing the inky shell.

Grit and dirt of the old floorboards shift against my fingertips as I move closer to the shining black egg.

Prayers like I've never said before stream through my

mind to whatever goddess my mother loved so much. I pray hard, wishing like hell the little creature will survive the heat and grow stronger from the kiss of the fire.

The smallest of lines crack against the surface, making me gasp.

The heat stings my cheeks as I peer into the heart of the embers.

A breath is long forgotten in my lungs.

Without blinking, I stare hard with impatience.

Sharp nails pierce through the shell, thrusting through it until its whole leg is revealed and ripping off the imprisonment of its small home.

A quiet but powerful hum of a roar reverberates through the egg. Strong wings burst from its remaining surroundings, and the tiny creature looks up at me with crystal-like eyes. Curiosity is in its gaze as it studies me for several seconds.

I shuffle quickly, reaching up on the table until I find the only food I have. I rip the meat into a thin shred, and with careful movements, I extend the offering to the little beast.

"Eat," I say in a quiet, gentle voice. It's a tone I'd never use with humans. As deadly as a dragon might be, humans are far worse creatures.

Yes, animals are much easier to speak with.

Bobble, the white tumid fish on my bedside table watches the beast with wide fearful eyes. His gaze is more bulging than normal if that's possible. The fat little fish looks like its puffy body is filled entirely with anxiety in this moment.

The dragon crawls out of the flames, shaking off the ash once it's on the floor next to me. A ticking sound announces its small steps as its talons hit the boards. Its head is the size of my palm, and its sharp teeth rake against my fingertips as it nibbles cautiously at the strip of dry meat in my hand.

Warm, golden firelight flashes across its eyes, and I lean in even closer to the creature. One eye is a pale blue, and one is a warm honey color. It's unique and beautiful. I've seen the iris mutation in dogs, but it isn't common. It keeps its gaze locked on me as it tears off more meat with razor-like teeth.

"My name's Arlow." I whisper the introduction with affection tinging my tone. It doesn't acknowledge me at all as it continues to devour its dinner. "Time for your friends."

With care, I cradle the red egg in my palms. The heat of the flames nips at my skin as I push it into the hot embers.

The second one is born just like the first.

It climbs out with more strength than the other dragon. Crimson scales capture the light of the fire in gleaming magnificence. It's just as deadly and beautiful as the other one, but it's not nearly as trusting. I can't even get close enough to offer it a strip of meat without the beast snapping its traitorous snout at me. I toss the food to the floor, and its taloned wing pulls the meat closer. Low growls emit from its throat with every move I make.

"Aren't you a little darling." I roll my eyes at its shitty attitude and begin bringing the last one over to the fireplace.

The white one is a little smaller than the others. It's so pure looking I can't bring myself to toss it into the flames. On my knees, I lean into the fire. I don't release the egg even as the heat stings my knuckles.

The embers crackle as I settle the egg in against the ash and dust.

What if it doesn't do as well? It's so small, what if it isn't ready yet?

I peek down at the two dragons ripping viciously at the last few scraps of meat.

Hell, what if these things kill me before the end of the week?

Life is filled with what-ifs.

You can only leap into the flames and hope you have the strength to walk away from the ash.

Heat washes over me as I lean into the warm fire. The golden hue of the flames glistens against my dark hair reflecting in the shimmering white surface.

Just when my hope starts to sink low in my stomach, a small crack shatters down the curved shell. The cracking sound sparks excitement all through me.

And just like that, another beautiful monster is born.

Order *Taming* and start the complete sexy series today!

ALSO BY A.K. KOONCE

Reverse Harem Books

Origins of the Six

Academy of Six

Control of Five

Destruction of Two

Wrath of One

The Hopeless Series

Hopeless Magic

Hopeless Kingdom

Hopeless Realm

Hopeless Sacrifice

The To Tame a Shifter Series

Taming

Claiming

Maiming

Sustaining

Reigning

The Villainous Wonderland Series

Into the Madness

Within the Wonder

Under the Lies

The Royal Harem Series

The Hundred Year Curse

The Curse of the Sea

The Legend of the Cursed Princess

The Severed Souls Series

Darkness Rising

Darkness Consuming

Darkness Colliding

The Huntress Series

An Assassin's Death

An Assassin's Deception

An Assassin's Destiny

Stand Alone Contemporary Romance

Hate Me Like You Do

Paranormal Romance

The Cursed Kingdoms Series

The Cruel FAe King

The Cursed Fae King

The Crowned Fae Queen

The Mortals and Mystics Series

Fate of the Hybrid, Prequel

When Fate Aligns, Book one

When Fate Unravels, Book two

When Fate Prevails, Book three

Resurrection Island

ABOUT A.K. KOONCE

A.K. Koonce is a USA Today bestselling author. She's a mom by day and a fantasy and paranormal romance writer by night. She keeps her fantastical stories in her mind on an endless loop while she tries her best to focus on her actual life and not that of the spectacular, but demanding, fictional characters who always fill her thoughts.

Printed in Great Britain
by Amazon